THE ARABIAN NIGHTS

OR TALES TOLD BY SHEHEREZADE DURING A THOUSAND NIGHTS AND ONE NIGHT

rendered into English by

BRIAN ALDERSON

and embellished by

MICHAEL FOREMAN

LONDON
VICTOR GOLLANCZ LTD
1992

For Sheherezade herself

Asie, Asie, Asie,
Vieux pays merveilleux des contes de nourrice . . .

First published in Great Britain 1992
by Victor Gollancz Ltd
14 Henrietta Street, London WC2E 8QJ
Text copyright © Brian Alderson 1992
Illustrations copyright © Michael Foreman 1992

The right of Brian Alderson and Michael Foreman
to be identified as authors of this work
has been asserted by them in accordance with the
Copyright, Designs and Patents Act 1988

A catalogue record for this book
is available from the British Library

ISBN 0 575 04251 6

Photoset in Great Britain by
Rowland Phototypesetting Ltd, Bury St Edmunds, Suffolk
Printed in Hong Kong by Imago Publishing Ltd

CONTENTS

In the name of
ALLAH
the All-compassionate

Praise be to Him
the Beneficent King,
Creator of the Universe,
Lord of the Three Worlds,
who set up the Unpillared Firmament

and who stretched out the Earth even as a Bed;

and Grace and Blessings be upon the Lord

MOHAMMED

Divine Apostle
may his Name live until the
Day of Doom

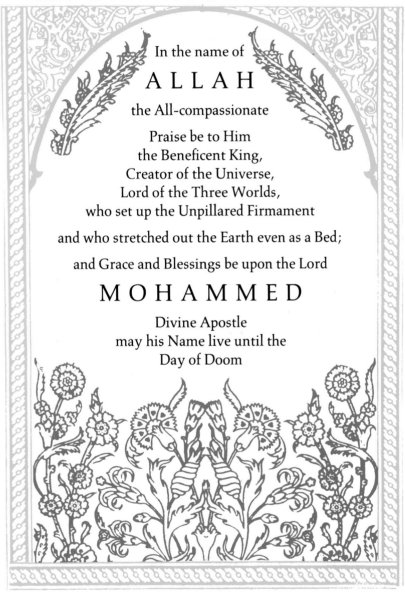

THE TWO KINGS, SHAH SHAHRYAR AND SHAH ZAMAN, AND THE WAZIR'S DAUGHTER SHEHEREZADE

In past times, in the far history of the world there was a great king who ruled over all the lands of Arabia and Persia, even to the shores of India, and when this king died he left his kingdom to his two sons, Shahryar and Zaman. These brothers were as close to one another as the nut within its shell and they divided their inheritance equally between them; Shahryar becoming king of land towards the west, with his palace at Baghdad, and Zaman becoming king of lands towards the east, with his palace at Samarkand.

For many years the brothers ruled their two kingdoms with justice and mercy until one day the Shah Shahryar felt a longing to see the Shah Zaman once more, so he called to him his chief minister, or Wazir, and he ordered that a great caravan be prepared to journey to his brother. There were to be camels and horses, laden with rich gifts of jewels and silks, there were to be white slaves and brown slaves, bearing precious ointments and sweetmeats, and in their midst the Wazir should journey with a letter full of loving greetings, in which the Shah Shahryar invited the Shah Zaman to return to Baghdad to be his honoured guest.

All came to pass as the Shah Shahryar intended. The Wazir and the caravan of horses and camels and body slaves brought the letter to the Shah Zaman, and after a week of feasting the Shah Zaman prepared a like baggage train to travel to his brother's palace. Loaded with many presents of gold and ivory, with rich carpets and with hangings of brocade, the caravan assembled and amid the rejoicings of the people of Samarkand it left the great gate of the city and encamped the first night within view of the city walls.

Now it so happened that, in the deepest part of the night, the Shah Zaman awoke in his tent and recollected that he had left

in his chamber in his palace a great ruby that was to be a present from himself to his brother. So he secretly arose and made his way back to the city, gaining entrance to the palace through a private postern, and climbing by a hidden staircase to his own chamber. What should be his horror however, when, on entering the room, he beheld his wife sleeping in the arms of a giant slave on his own carpet-bed.

"By Allah!" cried the Shah to himself, "how can it be that such a thing can happen, with the baggage train even yet within sight of the city walls? And if it can happen thus, what else may take place during the time that I am at my brother's court?" And in rage and sorrow he drew his scimitar and with one blow sliced the sleeping lovers into four pieces. Then he seized the forgotten ruby from its place and returned to his encampment in secret as he had come.

With expectation and longing the caravan now travelled its way across the mountains and the deserts to the city of Baghdad where it was greeted by the lords and the people alike, and the Shah Shahryar himself came down to open the city gates for his brother and to lead him in honour to the imperial palace. But through all the journeyings and the rejoicings the Shah Zaman was cast down, unable to think of anything beyond the death of love and the faithlessness of humankind. And although his brother prepared for him a great feast—the first in a long line of feasts—and although he was lodged in a wing of the palace resplendent with rich hangings and carpets and overlooking the Shah's own pleasure garden, there could be no raising his despondent spirits. His eye paled and his skin turned yellow with grief and nothing that his brother could do would revive him. "I am tired after my long journey," was all that he would say.

One day it came about that the Shah Shahryar prepared a great hunting expedition. Hoping that it would distract his brother from his sorrows he called upon him to mount and join them in the chase. But the Shah Zaman refused, asking only to be allowed to rest, and so the king and his huntsmen departed and left him to be cared for in his own quarter of the palace.

As he made his way dolefully from room to room it so happened that he came upon a little lattice window overlooking a secluded glade of the Shah's pleasure garden. Peering out through a corner of the window he was surprised to see the Shah's wife, who was a woman of great beauty, traversing the lawns, surrounded by a company of twenty slave girls in their robes and hoods. When they reached a fountain in the centre of the glade they cast off their robes and behold! they were not all slave girls, but girls and men too, and as they began to disport themselves naked beside the water the captain of the slave-guard leapt from a nearby tree and joined with the Queen herself.

In amazement the Shah Zaman watched the secret joys of the Queen and her slaves. "Truly," he said to himself, "the trustlessness and depravity of man stretches even to Baghdad!" and from that time on he began to recover his spirits. His eye brightened, his walk took on a new vigour, and when his brother returned from the hunt he was surprised and delighted at the change that he saw.

"Alhamdohlillah!" he cried, "when I departed the flower was fading, when I came back the flower was flourishing. What is the meaning of this riddle?" But the Shah Zaman kept his own counsel, not wishing that his brother too should be cast into the despair that had been his.

As the days passed however, the Shah Shahryar would not let the matter rest. He urged and urged his brother to tell him the reason for the sudden reversal of his fever and eventually the Shah Zaman gave way and told everything: the faithlessness of his wife, the killing of the wretched pair, the discovery that the Queen of Shah Shahryar was faithless too.

"By Allah!" cried the Shah, "can such a thing be possible?" And once more he ordered a hunting party to be prepared, and one which this time both he and his brother would attend; so the next day they set off for the chase. This time though, at their first encampment, the Shahs Shahryar and Zaman left their Wazirs to guard their tents, with orders that none should be admitted on pain of death, and they returned in secret to the palace. There, the next day, they placed themselves by the lattice window and observed how, once more, the Shah's wife and the slave-guard, the slaves and the handmaidens took their pleasure in the pleasure garden.

"Truly, my brother," cried the Shah Shahryar in despair, "there is no faith to be found in humankind. Let us betake ourselves from this evil place, to walk the world as poor pilgrims, never to return unless we should find one who is more wretchedly treated than ourselves. Then shall our wrath be without appeasement."

So the two Shahs left the palace and the hunting camp, where the Wazirs still stood their guard, and they walked as pilgrims across the world. Eventually they came to the line of the sea and here they took their rest in the shade of a tall tree beside a brook that ran down into the ocean.

While they were sitting there a great cloud began to form across the horizon and before long it took the shape of a huge black Jinni, or earth spirit, whirling towards them with the noise of a thousand hurricanes. In terror the two Shahs climbed into the branches of the tree where they had been sitting, and they beheld how the Jinni swirled down to the shore below them, carrying with him a huge chest made of crystal. This chest he opened, taking from it a broad casket locked with seven padlocks, and these locks he opened with a steel key, and out of the casket there stepped a girl as serenely beautiful as the sailing moon.

"Love of my heart," said the Jinni, "I would sleep." And she

knelt down on the sandy shore, and the Jinni placed his head on her lap and fell at once into a deep sleep.

When she saw that he truly was asleep she looked up into the tree and commanded the two kings to come down or else she would wake the Jinni who was with her. In fear and trembling Shah Shahryar and his brother descended to the ground, and then, gently moving from the sleeping Jinni, she commanded that each of them should come to her as a man comes to his wife. In vain they protested, in vain they sought to escape; there was nothing for it but to do as she required, under pain of her waking the Jinni.

When she had had her way with them she demanded that each should give her the ring of office that he carried on his finger, and when they had done so she went to her casket and drew from it a string on which were knotted five hundred and seventy of such similar rings. "You should know," she said, fastening their tokens in place, "that this Jinni snatched me away for himself the night I was to be married and he keeps me locked within my casket in a chest of crystal at the bottom of the sea, so that none but he may enjoy me. Even so—such is my cunning—I have betrayed him no less than five hundred and seventy—now five hundred and seventy-two times, and here is my proof. But go your way now, my Lords, before this creature should awake and slay us all."

So the Shah Shahryar and the Shah Zaman left the Jinni and his lady beside the line of the sea, and the Shah Shahryar said, "Is not this Jinni more wretched than ourselves? Just as he is more mighty, so his humiliation is the greater at the hands of this woman. Let us return to the palace and take our just revenge." And the two Shahs made their way back to the hunting camp, and returned to the palace with all their train, and the Shah Shahryar ordered forthwith that his faithless wife should be done to death. He then swore a great oath, that, from that day on, he would every night marry a new bride and every morning he would slay her, and so he would be avenged on the faithlessness of women.

Thus it came about. Every night a girl was brought to the bridal bed with great pomp, and every dawn the Wazir was called to lead her to her execution; but it was not long before the people began to cry out at such cruelty. Men hid their daughters, or carried them over the sea to other lands, for fear that they should become brides of the Shah Shahryar, until eventually the Wazir could find no girl to bring to the Sultan. The only ones left in all the city were the Wazir's own two daughters, Sheherezade and Dunyazad.

Now Sheherezade was a girl of quick wits, richly versed in the lore and fables of Arabia, and when she saw her father cast down and fearful for his life, because there was no bride for the king, she said, "By Allah, O my father, do not grieve, but send me to be partner to the Shah Shahryar. Either I shall live, or I shall die a death for all women, and whichever happens there should be nothing but pride for you." And however strongly the Wazir urged her not to be so foolish, the more strongly Sheherezade determined to pursue her course.

So in heavy dejection the Wazir took his way to the Shah's throne room and casting himself before his master's feet he revealed the intention of his daughter. "Wonder upon wonders!" cried the Shah, "how can this be? My oath is an oath for all time and all women. It cannot be denied for the favours of my Wazir's daughter." For he had long known and loved Sheherezade and had no desire to visit on her the punishment of all the others. But the Wazir wept and told him that she was not to be diverted from her aim—that she must and would marry the Shah and die the death of her kind; and the Shah, with admiration for her comeliness and for her courage, bade his servants prepare the wedding feast, and bade his headsman test his sharpest axe, that her death in the morning should be swift and sure.

But Sheherezade rejoiced in her fate and called to her younger sister, Dunyazad.

"Listen well, O sister," she said. "Tonight I go to the Sultan Shahryar to be his bride and his wife. Now after he has taken me to the marriage bed I will send for you to be with me—for at dawn I shall be beheaded—and you must say to me, 'Tell me, O sister, for the night is long and we cannot sleep, some story that will while away the hours before the sad sunrise', and then I shall tell a tale which, Allah willing, shall be the saving of us all."

"With all my heart," said Dunyazad. And so it came to pass that the Wazir brought Sheherezade to the Shah and they were

married, and in all joy he brought her to the marriage bed where, after much pleasure, they fell asleep. But in the middle of the night Sheherezade woke and called upon her husband, saying, "My Lord, I cannot sleep for fear of the daylight hour when I shall lose my life. Permit me to send for Dunyazad, my sister, that she may be with me in this time of trial." So the Shah gave his leave, and when Dunyazad came she said, "Tell me, O sister, for the night is long and we cannot sleep, some story that will while away the hours before the sad sunrise."

"If my Lord permits," said Sheherezade; and the Shah—who dearly loved a tale—agreed, and so Sheherezade began the tale of:–

THE FISHERMAN AND THE JINNI

I have heard, O auspicious King, that there was once an aged fisherman who lived in great poverty with his wife and six children. Each day he would go down to the sea-shore to fish and it was his habit to cast his net into the water three times and three times only.

So one afternoon he went down to the tide-line, set down his basket, waded into the sea and cast his net. When it had settled to the bottom he gathered the cords together and tried to haul it in, but however much he pulled it would not budge an inch, so he drove a stake into the ground, fastened the cords of the net to it and dived into the water to see what the burden was. Eventually he released the net and brought it to land, only to discover that all it contained was a dead jackass which had torn the meshes.

"Truly," said the fisherman, "there is no Majesty and there is no Might save in Allah, but this is strange winnings to get from the sea," and he cast his net a second time. Once more he brought it to land only with great difficulty, diving to free the burdened net from the sea-bottom. And once more he found that it contained not a shoal of fish but rubbish—a large pitcher full of sand and mud, potsherds and broken glass.

"Lord!" cried the fisherman, "You know that I cast my net only three times in each day. Twice have I cast now and You have rendered me nothing; pray give me my daily sustenance." And calling again upon Allah he threw his net the third time and watched as it sank and settled.

But this cast was no different from the others. The net stuck and there was nothing for it, but the fisherman had to dive down and free its tangles from the bottom—and this time when he brought it to land he found that it contained a jar of brass, shaped like a cucumber and stoppered with a leaden cap that bore the seal of the Emperor Solomon, the son of David.

"Praise and blessings to Allah!" cried the fisherman, "for here is a fish that will bring me ten golden dinars in the brass market. But first I must know what riches it may contain." And he took out his knife and worked at the sealed stopper till he had loosened it from the jar. Then he carefully tipped the vessel to see what might be inside.

There was nothing. But as he gazed at the jar, marvelling greatly that Solomon or his agents should have sealed it without anything inside, he saw issue from the neck a black smoke which began to pour out across the surface of the shore and then to billow heavenward in a huge, thick vapour. And slowly the vapour condensed into a shape and the shape into the solid figure of a Jinni whose crest touched the clouds while his feet were yet planted on the

ground. His head was as a dome, his hands like pitchforks, his legs long as mizzen masts, his mouth big as a cave, his teeth like tombstones and his eyes burning like two brilliant lamps.

"There is no God but *the* God!" cried the Jinni, "be of good cheer, O fisherman!"

But the fisherman, far from being of good cheer, was shaking in his shoes. His teeth chattered, the spittle dried in his mouth and he became blind about what to do.

"Why biddest thou me to be of good cheer?" he asked.

"Because in this very hour thou must die a chosen death."

"Whyso?" cried the fisherman. "Why shouldst thou kill me, who have brought thee up out of the sea to dry land and freed thee from thy jar?"

"Ask not," said the Jinni. "Ask only by what kind of death thou seekest to die and by what manner of slaughter I shall slay thee. For thou must know that I am one of the Jann that sinned against Solomon, the son of David, and that when I refused to embrace the True Faith he shut me up in that jar and had me cast into the midmost ocean.

"Know also, fisherman, that I lay in that ocean an hundred years, and I said in my heart, 'Whoso shall release me, him will I enrich for ever and ever,' but no one came. So I lay there four hundred years more, and I said in my heart, 'Whoso shall release me, to him I will grant three wishes,' but still and still and still nobody came. Thereupon I waxed wroth with exceeding wrath and I swore to myself that whoso should release me, him would I slay, giving him only the choice of death that he should die."

But with this speech of the Jinni, Sheherezade perceived the coming of the day and fell silent.

"What a strange tale this is," said her sister Dunyazad.

"Indeed so," said Sheherezade, "but it is as nothing to what must follow if my Lord will permit me to live until the coming night and will spare me from his wrath."

And the Sultan said to himself, "By Allah, I shall not kill her until the tale be told." So he went forth into his court. He gave edicts and he granted suits, and when his Wazir came to him with a shroud made for Sheherezade he said no word but left the hall. And when night came he joined Sheherezade once more in the marriage bed.

After they had caroused and slept, and when the first part of the night was over, Dunyazad came to them once more, saying,

"O my sister, continue now thy story of the Fisherman and the Jinni." And without more ado Sheherezade went on:–

It hath reached me, O auspicious King, that the Jinni had held forth in a long speech, threatening death to the fisherman. But during his words the fisherman gradually resumed his senses and determined in his mind that, as a man of contrivance and intelligence, he might yet encompass the destruction of the Contumacious One.

"Then is it so," he asked, "that my only injury toward thee is that I let thee out of thy brass bottle?"

"That is so," said the Jinni.

"Then is it so," he asked again, "that for the good I have done thee thou returnest only evil?"

"Indeed it is so," said the Jinni, "but I have endured enough of this talk. Die thou must, and without delay."

"Then tell me," cried the fisherman, "by the Most Great Name, graven on the seal of Solomon, the son of David, if I question thee on one more matter wilt thou give me a true answer?"

"Yea," answered the Jinni (for he trembled at the mention of the Most Great Name), "but ask it briefly."

"Very well," said the fisherman. "Tell me, however was it that thou couldst fit into this brass jar which would not now hold even the toenail of thy big toe?"

"What?" said the Jinni, "dost thou not believe that I was trapped in that bottle a thousand years or more?"

"Nay," said the fisherman, "how could I believe it, when I see that thou ridest above me in the clouds and this jar so small? Thou couldst not do it."

So at that the Jinni shook himself and became again a black vapour and shrank and little by little flowed back into the jar; and when he was well inside the fisherman sprang for the stopper and the seal and stoppered up the mouth of the jar, crying out, "A boon! A boon! Ask me by what kind of death thou seekest to die and by what manner of slaughter I shall slay thee; for by Allah, I will throw thee into the sea and will post a warning to all that come here that in these waters there dwells a Jinni who gives as a favour a choice of death to those who rescue him!"

Now when the Jinni realized that he had been outwitted and was once more under the seal of Solomon he became lowly and submissive.

"I did but jest," he said, speaking through the sides of the jar.

"Thou liest," said the fisherman, "thou vilest of the Jann. There is nothing for it but I shall throw thee back into the sea where thou mayst be housed and homed another thousand years . . .''

"Ah!'' cried the Jinni, "say not so. Open for me and I shall serve thee well.''

"Thou liest!'' said the fisherman. "It will be no better with thee than it was with the Wazir of King Yunan and the Sage Duban.''

"And who was the Wazir of King Yunan and the Sage Duban?'' asked the Jinni; and there followed:–

THE TALE WHICH THE FISHERMAN
TOLD OF THE SAGE DUBAN

Know thou, O Jinni, that in ages long past there was a King in Persia by the name of Yunan. He was a powerful ruler, but his body was afflicted with leprosy and although doctors and physicians and leeches came from every nation, with medicines and powders and unguents, not one of them could cure the King.

Now one day there came to the land an ancient sage who was called Duban, a man versed in the books of Greece and Rome, and of Persia, Arabia and Syria, one who knew all the skills of healing with herbs and potions. Nor was it long before he heard of the sufferings of the King, and after a night of contemplation he betook himself to the court, where he knelt before the King and kissed the ground between his hands.

"O King," he said, "tidings have reached me of your misfortune and of how a great host of physicians have found no way to mitigate it. But lo! I can cure thee, even though I make thee drink no draught nor anoint thee with no ointment."

And when King Yunan heard these words he marvelled greatly and said, "By Allah, if thou make me whole I will enrich thee down to the sons of thy sons, and I will give thee rich gifts and call thee friend."

So the sage took his way and hired a house in the city for the better storage of his books and scrolls and his medicines and aromatic roots. And there he fashioned a wonderful polo mallet with a curiously-wrought wooden handle, and he took the mallet to the King and brought him to the palace yard, there to play a chukka of polo. "Take the mallet," said Duban to the King, "and grip it as I do, so! Then ride into the game and strike the ball mightily up and down and as the palm of thy hand sweats upon the mallet so shall the cure be proved."

Then the King rode his pony into the polo match and played a vigorous chukka, striking the ball from one end of the ground to the other and sweating like any common man. And when the chukka was done he betook himself to the bath house and as he bathed he observed his body and saw that it was clean as virgin silver. The leprosy had gone.

 At this point Sheherezade once more left off her story, for the day was dawning. But once more the Sultan spared her life for the sake of the tale that she was telling. And the next night she continued:—

It hath reached me, O auspicious King, that the fisherman was telling the Jinni the tale of how the Sage Duban had come to King Yunan and cured him of his leprosy. Great was the rejoicing of King Yunan and of his court at this miraculous cure and when the Sage Duban appeared for an audience the King greeted him with due honour, set before him gifts of jewels and money and fine robes and treated him as friend.

But not everyone at the court was filled with such delight. For there was among the King's Wazirs, a Wazir of frightful aspect, shrunken with envy and malice, and when he saw the honours bestowed upon the Sage Duban his jealousy knew no bounds. That night he came before the King privily in his chamber and laid charges against the sage, that he was plotting the downfall of the King.

"How can this be?" said King Yunan. "Why, the sage cured me of my illness without drowning me in draughts or boiling me in ointments. How should I not reward him? Indeed, if I were to heed your warning and have him done to death I would surely repent of the deed as King Sindibad repented of killing his falcon."

"Pardon me, O King," said the Wazir, "but I know nothing of King Sindibad or of his falcon." So King Yunan recounted:—

THE TALE OF THE LOYAL FALCON

There was once a King of the Kings of Persia who loved hunting. He had reared a falcon, whom he took with him everywhere, and he had made for this falcon a golden cup which was hung about her neck that he might himself give her to drink therefrom.

Now one day the King and his men were out hunting and as they were staking their nets there came towards them a proud gazelle. "Stay!" cried the King, "whosoever allows that gazelle to spring over his head, that man shall I surely slay." But the gazelle advanced slowly towards the King himself, and when she reached him she sank back on her haunches, and crossed her forehoof over her breast as though to salute the King. And as he bowed in acknowledgement she suddenly bounded high over his head and sped off into the desert.

"By Allah!" cried the King, "my life is upon my own head!" and he galloped off in pursuit of the gazelle with his falcon on his fist. The chase carried them to the foothills of a row of mountains where the gazelle made for a cave in the rocks, but the King unleashed his falcon who swooped upon it and drove her talons into its head so that the King was able to come up and slay the beast with his mace; and after he had quartered it he packed it into his saddle bags and set off to return to his men.

By now though, it was the hottest time of the day, and both the King and his horse were athirst, so they sought about among the foothills for water. Nor was it long before they heard a plashing noise and found a tree which was dropping water as though it were melted butter.

At once the King took the golden cup from about his falcon's neck and filled it with the water; but before he could drink the bird struck with her pounces

and upset the lot. So the King filled the cup a second time, and again the bird overturned it with her talons. At this the King was wroth with exceeding wrath and when his falcon tipped the cup a third time he pulled out his sword and struck off one of her wings.

At this the creature raised its head and seemed to motion to the King to look up at the tree, and when he did so he saw there, enmeshed in the branches, a brood of vipers from whose fangs had dropped the streams that he took to be water. So without more ado he rode back to his camp with the slain gazelle, but when he came to attend to his injured bird it turned up its eyes at him and died.

"Thus," said King Yunan to his Wazir, "thus does ingratitude foster calamity, just as it did in the case of the husband and the parrot."

"Pardon me, O King," said the Wazir, "but I know nothing of the husband and the parrot." So King Yunan proceeded to tell:–

THE TALE OF THE FAITHFUL PARROT

There was once a certain merchant who married a woman of perfect beauty. "Happy for him," you may say, but because of her loveliness he was mad jealous that she might come to know some other man, so he kept to his house with her day and night.

Eventually, however, it came about that he must attend to business in a distant city, so he went to the bird market and bought for an hundred dinars a speaking parrot whom he put in the house to watch over his wife and to report to him when he returned.

Now his wife had indeed fallen in love with another man—a young Turk—and once the husband had gone he came to join her and they feasted by day and slept together by night. So when the merchant returned home he questioned the parrot about what had been going on and the bird told everything.

At once rage and violence entered the merchant's heart and he thrashed his wife as though she had been a dog in the street, and she, in her turn, called up her slave girls to punish whomsoever (as she believed), had told tales about her. But the slave girls all swore that they had kept her secret and they pointed to the parrot as the cause of all the trouble.

So the next time that the merchant went from home his wife made different plans, and before her lover arrived she arranged for the girls to attend around the parrot's cage. One sat underneath it with a hand-mill, grinding and grinding for all she was worth. One stood over the cage sprinkling water through its roof. And one ran about the room flashing the lamplight into the cage with mirrors of polished steel.

Thus, when the husband returned, he inquired of the parrot what might have happened in his absence, and the bird replied, "Pardon, O my master, but I can tell you nothing by reason of the thunder and lightning and pouring rain that assailed me all night."

"How can this be?" cried her master, "for we are in the season of high summer and there is neither cloud nor rain the whole time long." And with that he deemed that a bird who could lie once might lie twice and he hauled the parrot from its cage and dashed its brains out on the floor. Only later, when a slave girl confessed, did he discover the trick that had been placed on the bird and he mourned greatly that such faithfulness should be rewarded with death.

King Yunan's Wazir refused to be moved by these stories however and he continued day and night to turn the King's mind against the Sage Duban. "For after all," said he, "if he cured thee by so innocent a means as holding a polo stick, who is to say that he may not choose his time and slay thee with a like simplicity?''

And as water will wear rock, so these speeches wore away the King's faith in the Sage Duban and eventually he sent for him to attend his court.

''Knowest thou why I have summoned thee?'' he said; and the sage answered, ''Allah alone, the Most High, knows the secrets of the heart.''

''I have summoned thee only to take thy life and utterly destroy thee.''

''O King, wherefore so; and what ill have I done?''

''Men tell me that thou art a spy come hither to slay me, and lo! I will kill thee ere I be killed by thee.'' And the King called forth his Sworder to strike off the sage's head. But the sage pleaded that he might be spared (said the fisherman to the Jinni, 'Even as I pleaded with you when I let you out of the jar'), but the King was adamant: ''There is no help for it; die thou must, and without delay.''

Now when the sage realized that there was no turning the King from his purpose, he said, ''O King, if truly there be no help, then grant me some little time that I may go down to my house and make all preparations against my death, and on my return I will bring thee a parting gift that is the rarest of all rarities and that shall be a treasure for your treasury.''

''And what may that be?'' asked the King.

''It is a book that shall reveal to thee all the secrets of the world. For if—when thou hast cut my head off—thou open three leaves of the book and read three lines of the page on thy left hand, my head shall speak and shall answer every question thou choose to ask.''

Well, the King wondered much at this strange present and he sent the sage, closely guarded, to his house and all was settled as he desired. And the next day the King went to his audience hall, among his Emirs and his Wazirs, his Nabobs and his Chamberlains, and the Sage Duban stood before him bearing a worn old volume and a little flask of metal full of powder.

''Give me a tray,'' he said, and when they brought him one he spread the powder on it, smoothed it out, and said, ''O King, take this book but do not open it until my head falls; then set it on the powder of this tray and forthwith the blood will cease to flow and the time will be at hand to open the book.''

So the King took the objects and made a sign to the Sworder, who struck off the head of the Sage Duban and placed it on the tray. Straightway the blood stopped flowing and the head unclosed its eyes and said, ''Now open the book, O King.''

The King opened the book, but found that the leaves were stuck together; so he licked his finger and turned the first leaf. There was no writing to be seen. So with much difficulty and in the same way he opened six leaves of the book,

but could find nothing on them.

"O Physician," he said, "there is no writing here."

"O King," said the head, "turn over yet more." And so the King proceeded, licking his finger at each leaf to separate it from its fellows. On all the pages he found neither guidance nor wisdom—but on all of them his finger discovered, unbeknown, a rare and subtle poison and within minutes of his having opened the book the King fell into violent convulsions.

"*So ends the pride of mortal things,*" said the head.

"*So ends the tyranny of Kings.*"

And it spoke no more.

"Thus you may see, O Jinni," said the fisherman, "that if King Yunan had spared the Sage Duban, Allah would have spared him. Likewise if thou hadst spared me then Allah would have spared thee; but nothing would satisfy thee save my death; so now I will render thee the same service and cast thee back into the ocean, with warnings to whomsoever shall find thee to toss thee back again, and thou shalt abide in these waters till the End of Time."

Then began a great argument between the fisherman, shouting on the shore, and the Jinni, booming in his brass jar. And the end of it was that the Jinni swore a solemn oath by Allah, the Most High, that if the fisherman released him, so far from slaughtering him he would reward him with an abundance of riches.

Once more therefore the fisherman lifted the stopper from the jar and the Jinni flared into the air like a smoke. Then, when he had once more resumed his gigantic state he kicked the brass jar with its stopper and seal and sent it flying an hundred miles into the sea. At this the fisherman feared once more for his life and trembled so that he wet his britches, but the Jinni laughed like the roaring of a tribe of desert lions and bade the fisherman follow him into the hills that lay at the back of the sea-shore.

There he took him into a hidden pass that led to a secret lake where fish were to be seen so thick that those on the surface were lying on the fins of those below.

"Here thou mayst fish in peace," said the Jinni, "and with thy three casts a day bring home neither jackasses, nor broken pots nor brass bottles, but a wealth of merchandise." And with that he made off to see the world that he had not seen for a thousand years while the fisherman lived to enjoy a long and prosperous life.

Now this tale of the fisherman and the Jinni was concluded during the fourth night of Sheherezade's storytelling, and because there was yet more time before the day dawned she went on to begin:–

THE TALE OF THE PORTER OF BAGHDAD

Who carried a great basket of provisions to the house of three wealthy ladies in the city and for his reward, he was allowed to stay and drink and eat with them and disport with them naked as they took their evening bath. And as Sheherezade told this story to the Shah

Shahryar the nights passed by and turned themselves to days, and
Sheherezade continually embroidered her tale so that:
the porter and the three ladies were joined by three Persian Kalandars (which
is to say Holy Men who live by begging), and each of these Kalandars had only
one eye;

and the porter and the ladies and the one-eyed Kalandars were then joined by
none other than the Caliph Harun-al-Rashid, and his Wazir, and Masrur his
Swordsman—all in disguise—who were walking through the town in quest of
adventures,

and the ladies prevailed upon the three Kalandars to tell the company how
each had come to lose his eye. Thus:
The First Kalandar lost his eye in revenge for an accident. For he was the son
of a king and one day, out hunting, he had shot an arrow into the eye of his
father's Wazir. Then, some years later, when that Wazir himself came to
power he caused the prince to be likewise blinded.

The Second Kalandar lost his eye through the violence of the Ifrit Jirjaris of the seed of Iblis. For he, too, was the son of a king, but by ill fortune he roused the wrath of the Ifrit who changed him into an ape. Only by the magical shape-shiftings of another emperor's daughter was he able to recover his form, but as he watched her battle with the Ifrit, the fire of their fury touched him and he was blinded in one eye.

The Third Kalandar lost his eye in the manner that Bluebeard's wives lost their heads. For in travelling the world he discovered a great palace, where dwelt forty damsels of amazing beauty. They made him welcome and entertained him as the king's son that he was, but after some time had passed they had, perforce, to leave him on his own for the space of forty days. They gave him keys to the doors of forty rooms in the palace, with injunctions that he might go into thirty-nine of them but not the fortieth. But pride and curiosity got the better of him and when he came to the fortieth door he opened it and found within a black horse of majestic size. This he mounted, and before he could command it, it flew off up into the air and carried him to a mountain far from the palace and there it left him—flicking out one of his eyes with its tail as it flew away.

Such were the stories told by the Kalandars to the Caliph of Baghdad and his servants and the three ladies and their porter, and they pleased their audience as much in the telling, as did Sheherezade the Shah Shahryar; and when those stories were done she went on to recite:–

THE TALE OF THE HUNCHBACK

His Lamentable Death

Once upon a time, long years ago, in a city in China there lived a hunchback who was court jester to the sultan of that place. One night he was walking through the streets when he fell in with a tailor and his wife—a jovial pair who liked any excuse for a party. So the tailor and his wife invited the hunchback home for supper and the tailor went down to the bazaar and laid in a stock of fried fish and bread and lemons and sweetmeats for dessert.

While they were feasting off these good things, the tailor's wife, by way of a joke, picked up a chunk of fish and stuffed it into the hunchback's mouth, saying:

> "Now, by Allah, swallow, swallow;
> If you do not, naught will follow,"

and the hunchback duly gulped it down. But the Lord looked not kindly on the joke. There was a bone stuck in the chunk of fish, which lodged in the hunchback's gullet, and without more ado he choked—and died.

Great was the consternation of the tailor and his wife. "Truly, there is no Majesty and no Might, save in Allah!" cried the man. "How should such foolishness fashion such a fate?" But his wife said, "Leave thy wailing, this is what we must do . . ." and she schemed a scheme by which they would wrap the hunchback in a silken shawl and carry him to the doctor's, crying all the while that he was an infant child overcome with plague.

So this they did and the people on the streets avoided them everywhere. And when they came to the doctor's house they knocked at the door and told the slave who answered it, that they had brought a child who was sick with an unknown sickness. "Here is a silver piece," they said, "go and tell thy master to come down at once," and while the slave girl hastened off they took the hunchback into the hallway, propped him up neatly at the top of the staircase and hurried home as fast as they could.

Now the doctor was at supper with his wife, but when he saw the silver piece that the slave girl brought him he jumped up and rushed to meet the customers who were like to prove such valuable patients; and bustling along in the dark he did not notice the hunchback's corpse leant up against the top of the stairs. He banged into it and straightway it tumbled over and rolled down to the bottom, flump!

"Lights!" he cried, "lights!"—and when the girl brought a lamp and he saw the hunchback lying there stone dead he believed that he had died from the fall. "By Hippocrates!" he said, "I have killed a hunchback," and he rushed back up the stairs to his wife, moaning and flapping his arms. "Leave thy blethering," she said, "all things can be turned to good account. We will carry him up to the terrace roof and lower him down into the dinner-man's garden, and the dogs will come down and eat him up."

For it so happened that the doctor and his wife lived next door to the reeve who had control over the sultan's kitchen, and this reeve—whom they liked to call the dinner-man, was wont to bring home great stores of oil and fat and leftover meat and sheep's tails which he stored in his garden, where he was thus much plagued by the local rats and mice and cats and dogs, who broke in to steal the food. So the doctor and his wife carried the dead hunchback up to their open roof and then carefully lowered him down into the dinner-man's garden, where they contrived to prop him against the wall of the shed where he stored his foodstuffs.

Before long the dinner-man returned home from an evening reading of the Koran and what should he see but a shadowy figure skulking by his store-room. "Wah! By Allah," he said, "so it is men that rob me;" and he seized a hammer and knocked the hunchback on the head, clunk! At once the hunchback fell over and the dinner-man shone a lamp on him and discovered to his horror that he must have knocked him dead. "Aieee!" he cried, "a curse upon all sheep's tails and hunchbacks. Was it not enough that thou shouldst be a man of crumpled stature, and must thou be a robber too? Alas, alas, may the Veiler of all Secrets be with me in this enterprise." And he picked up the hunchback and carried him through the dark of the night to the bazaar, where he leant him against a wall as though he were a drunkard resting on his homeward way.

Soon after, along came the sultan's steward (who was indeed drunk), and stopped by the wall to attend to some urgent business. But when he saw this figure looming beside him, he thought it to be an assassin and he straightway smote him. "Actions first, questions later," said he to himself. But no sooner had he struck the hunchback once than he toppled over and the steward fell upon him and began pummelling him and shouting for help.

This brought the watchman of the bazaar with his lamp and his cudgel, and even though the drunken steward explained the provocation he had suffered from a hunchback who sought to steal his turban and all his worldly goods, there was no doubt that the hunchback himself was dead. So the steward was taken away for trial and was condemned to be hanged that very morning.

The gallows were put up; the torch-bearer came, who was also the local hangman; the governor came to approve the execution; and a great crowd assembled to watch the fun. But no sooner was it revealed that the steward was to be hanged for killing the hunchback in the bazaar than the dinner-man came forward crying, "Stay! stay! it was not he who killed the hunchback; it was I," and he related how he had found the marauding fellow in his garden, lurking to steal his meat.

"Very well," said the governor to the torch-man, "change 'em round. Hang up this man on his own confession."

But no sooner was the dinner-man ready to be hanged than up came the doctor, crying, "Stay! stay! it was not he who killed the hunchback; it was I," and he told how he had knocked him down the staircase in his haste to lay hands on his clients' silver pieces.

"Very well," said the governor to the torch-man, "change 'em round. Hang up this man on his own confession."

But no sooner was the doctor ready to be hanged than up came the tailor crying, "Stay! stay! it was not he who killed the hunchback; it was I," and he related the sad joke of the chunk of fish.

"Very well," said the governor to the torch-man, "change 'em round. Hang up this man on his own confession."

But by this time the torch-man on the scaffold was getting a trifle weary of all the chopping and changing and was beginning to lose interest in hanging anyone that day; while up at the court the sultan was beginning to wonder what had become of his hunchback jester, for he'd done all his duties for the morning and wanted some amusement. So when they told him that his hunchback was down at the scaffold, stone dead, while the torch-bearer was put to a deal of trouble because so many people had claimed to have killed him, the sultan decided he was being deprived of some curious entertainment. So he sent for his chamberlain and bade him go down to the scaffold, pay off the torch-bearer, and bring the variety of murderers before him.

What Happened at the Sultan's Court

Well—
  There's no avail
  In a twice-told tale;
so we do not need to hear again the explanations that were given to the sultan, but when they were over he was mightily pleased and called for the whole to be written in letters of liquid gold. "For," said he, "did you ever hear a more

[39]

wondrous story than the four-times killing of my hunchback?"

Whether he meant the question for a statement or a challenge I do not know, but without more ado the sultan's steward came forward:

and the sultan's steward told what he took to be a wondrous story: a tale of a rich and handsome man who none the less stole gold for the love of a lady and lost his right hand thereby;

and he was followed by the dinner-man, who told what he took to be a wondrous story: a tale of a doctor of law, who gained entry to the harem of the Caliph Harun-al-Rashid and who married its stewardess, but who lost his thumbs and his big toes because he dared to make love to her while his hands were stained from eating garlic stew;

and he was followed by the doctor, who told what he took to be a wondrous story: a strange tale of love and jealousy, whereby the son of a merchant slept with the sister of his mistress and woke to find her murdered, and how he allowed his hand to be cut off rather than confess to what had happened.

And while all these tales pleased the sultan they seemed to him to be in no way so wondrous as the events concerning the hunchback, and it was left to the tailor to explain how, on the night when the hunchback died, he had first been to a marriage feast for one of his companions, which was attended by the guildsmen of the city: the tailors, the silk-spinners, the carpenters and so on.

Now in the course of the feasting there arrived a young man, of most handsome appearance, except that he was lame in one leg. As he came into the company, so he observed that among the guests there was a certain swarthy barber, and no sooner had he seen him than he turned and made to leave the feast, "For," said he, "I have sworn never to sit in the same place nor tarry in the same town as this black-faced barber of ill omen."

When he was prevailed upon to speak more of this matter it came to light that he had, some time before, been in love with one of the daughters of the great judge in Baghdad. By much contrivance he had arranged to be secretly transported into her chambers while her father was at prayers, but had determined first to be barbered and had therefore sent for the silentest and peaceablest barber who could be found in Baghdad. What should be his torment, however, when a barber came who claimed to be a silent man but who, at his own estimation, was:

an astrologer,
   an alchemist,
      a grammarian,
         a lexicographer,
           a logician,
              a rhetorician,
                a mathematician,
                  an astronomer,
                    a theologian,
and a Master of the Traditions of the Apostle and the Commentaries of the
Koran. Not only did this Silent Barber talk so much that the young man was
late for his assignation, but he was also so curious about the conduct of the
affair that he caused mayhem round the house of the great judge, with the
result that the young man was tipped out of a window and broke his leg. So
who should wonder that, through losing his lady and losing his limberness, he
should never wish to see the barber again.

    For his part, however, the barber gave token of the truth of all that the
young man said, first by telling the assembled company at the marriage feast
of his fame as a Silent Man and then by embarking upon six inconsequential
tales, one for each of his brothers: the Prattler, the Babbler, the Gabbler, the
Long-necked Gugglet, the Whiffler, and the Man of Many Clamours—as a
result of which the tailor and his friends locked the barber in a cupboard and
there let him rest till his tongue should have cooled down.

"In sooth," cried the sultan, "I should like to see this barber," and straightway he was sent for and released from his cupboard and came before the sultan, where were also to be found the tailor and the doctor and the dinner-man and the steward and the corpse of the hunchback. They explained to him how this audience had come into being to hear his adventures, but before he could ever begin, he looked round the faces of them all and then laughed till he fell over backwards.

"Truly," he said, "there is a wonder in every death, but the death of this hunchback is indeed worthy to be written in letters of liquid gold!" And he went over to where the corpse was lying and took from his barber's bag a little pot of ointment, with which he anointed the hunchback's throat, then he drew out the chunk of fish with its bone, all soaked in blood. Thereupon the hunchback sneezed, like one who has eaten raw horse-radish, and jumped up as if nothing had happened.

From that day forth he continued to jest before the sultan, just as the tailor tailored, the doctor doctored, the dinner-man dined, the steward stewed and the barber barbered until there came to them all, each in his turn, the Destroyer of Delights and the Sunderer of Societies.

And when Sheherezade had completed the Tale of the Hunchback she went on to tell more tales of the kings and princes of the land. She told too, out of her recollection, fables of the birds and beasts, among which was:—

THE FABLE OF THE BIRDS AND THE BEASTS AND THE CARPENTER

In times of yore a peacock lived with his wife on a piece of land beside the sea. But the place was infested with lions and all manner of wild beasts so the two birds sought for some other abode and eventually happened upon an island, verdant with trees and fresh with running streams.

Now while the birds were enjoying the fruits and the waters of their new home there came before them a duck, flapping its wings and crying in terror, "Beware, and again I say beware, of the Sons of Adam!" But the peacocks spoke comfortingly to the duck, saying that they would defend her against all creatures, and that anyway there could be no Sons of Adam upon this island.

"Alhamdohlillah!" cried the duck, "glory to God for your kindness, but you must know that the Sons of Adam have learned how to traverse the waters of the sea and that there is none like them for mischief and crafty cunning." And the duck went on to relate how one day she had been warned in a dream to flee the Sons of Adam and how in her wanderings she had come upon the whelp of a lion sitting at the door of a cave.

"Draw near," called the lion, "and tell me thy name and nature."

"My name is Duck, and I am of the bird-kind; and what of thee?"

"My name is Lion. My father hath warned me against those creatures named the Sons of Adam and I am seeking them across the world that I may kill them."

So Duck was glad to travel under the protection of Lion, and they had not gone very far before they saw a cloud of dust approaching them. As it came near they perceived at its centre a running naked ass, tearing across the land.

"Hark ye, crack-brain!" called Lion. "What is thy name and nature?"

"O Son of the Sultan, I am Ass and I am fleeing a Son of Adam."

"Whyso? Dost thou fear he will kill thee?"

"Nay, O Son of the Sultan, but I fear his cheating ways, for he hath a thing called a Pack-saddle which he setteth on my back, and a thing called Girths which he bindeth about my belly, and a thing called a Crupper which he putteth beneath my tail, and a thing called a Bit which he placeth in my

[43]

mouth; and he fashioneth a Goad to drive me to do his bidding and carry his wares. And when I can work no more he will kill me and cast me on the rubbish heap for dogs.''

''Fear not,'' said the lion whelp, ''for Duck and I will defend thee,'' and they continued on their way. They had not gone far before they saw another cloud of dust approaching them across the plain, and this proved to be a black horse with a silver blaze on his forehead.

''Come hither, majestic beast,'' called Lion, ''and tell us thy name and nature.''

''I am Horse of the horse-kind and I am fleeing a Son of Adam.''

''Whyso? How should so mighty a creature as thyself be afraid of a Son of Adam when one such as I is seeking only to meet and slay him? Surely one kick from one of thy hoofs would prevail against him?''

''Nay, O Prince,'' said Horse, ''do not be deluded; for he hath a thing called a Hobble which shall prevent me from doing so, and when he is minded to ride me he hath a Saddle and Girths and a Bit and a Rein with which to make me do

his bidding. Then when I grow old and can no longer run for him he will sell me to the miller to grind corn and the miller, in his turn, will sell me to the knacker, who will cut my throat and flay my hide, and pluck out my tail for the sieve-maker, and boil my fat for tallow candles.''

When the lion whelp heard these words his rage against this Son of Adam increased and he sought directions from Horse where they might find the creature; and before they had gone far they encountered a furious camel, gurgling and pawing the earth with his feet. This mighty beast the lion whelp took to be a Son of Adam, but before he could spring at him and tear him to pieces Duck explained that his name was Camel, and Camel explained that he was himself fleeing from a Son of Adam.

''Whyso? Surely with one kick of thy hoof thou wouldst slay him?''

''Nay, O Prince,'' said Camel, ''for he is a creature of wily ways and he putteth into my nostrils a twine of goat's hair called a Nose-ring, and over my head a thing called a Halter and he delivers me to the least of his children to

lead about the world; and when I am old and good for nothing he selleth me to the knacker who cuts my throat and makes over my hide to the tanners and my flesh to the cooks."

"Where didst thou leave this Son of Adam?" asked the lion whelp.

"Why, even now he cometh after me and I am away now to the wilds where he will not find me."

"Nay, O Camel, stay with us and thou wilt see how I shall tear him to pieces and crunch his bones and drink his blood . . ."

And as Lion was speaking there came towards them a little, old, bent, lean man, carrying on his shoulders a basket of carpenter's tools and on his head a branch of a tree and eight planks. When Lion saw him he walked towards him and the man smiled at him and said: "O King, who defendeth these creatures from harm, Allah prosper thy ways and strengthen thee, that thou mayst protect me too!"

"Whyso? What is thy name and nature—for assuredly thou art a beast the like of which I have never seen before and I would wish to aid thee, if only for the eloquence of thy words."

"O Lord of wild beasts, I am a carpenter, and I am journeying to thy father's wazir, the lynx, to make for him a shelter against the Sons of Adam. For he knows the ways of those creatures and he would have a house wherein he might dwell and fend off his enemies."

[46]

Now when he heard this the lion whelp grew envious of the lynx and he said to the carpenter, "By my life, I will have you make a house for me with those planks before ever you go to Sir Lynx."

"O Lord of wild beasts," said the carpenter, "that may not be. I will go first to the lynx and then return to thy service and build thee a house."

"By Allah," roared Lion, "thou shalt not leave this place till thou build me a house of planks!" and he sprang at the carpenter so that he fell over and his gear fell to the ground. "Yea; thou mayst in truth fear the Sons of Adam, O Carpenter, for thou art a feeble beast with no force to protect thee."

But the carpenter got up and smiled at Lion, saying, "Well, I will make for thee a house." And he took his planks and nailed together a dwelling in the form of a chest after the measure of a young lion. And he left one end free for a door and he took hammer and nails and said to Lion, "Enter the house through this opening, that I may fit it to thy measure."

So the whelp rejoiced that he had his way and he crept through the opening into the house. Once he was inside, the carpenter whipped the lid on to the opening and nailed it down.

"O Carpenter," cried Lion, "what is this narrow house thou hast made for me? Open the gate and let me out!"

"Alas!" said the carpenter, "I am but feeble and lacking in force and I know not what may befall me if I release you once more among these creatures here. Perhaps I shall send for the lynx, that he may inspect my capacities as a builder of houses."

And with that Ass and Horse and Camel—and even Duck—knew that this was a Son of Adam and they took their ways in haste lest the carpenter should build dwellings for them too.

And after telling that fable Sheherezade went on to tell how there are indeed no limits to greed and betrayal. Firstly she told:–

THE FABLE OF THE WOLF AND THE FOX

Some time ago a wolf and a fox set up house together. But the wolf was forever tyrannizing the fox, putting him in his place like a servant, buffeting him, and doing down all his offers of friendship. The fox smiled through it all though, but in his heart he said, "There is no help for it; I must encompass the destruction of this wolf."

Now one day the fox came upon a vineyard, and as he walked round it he saw a hole made in part of its wall. But experience had taught him to be wary of such pretty invitations and he crept carefully up to the hole and looked at it closely. And indeed it was a trap, for the owner of the vineyard had dug a deep pit beyond it, lightly covered with a mat of sticks, to catch whatever wild beasts were foolhardy enough to come in to the vineyard through the hole.

So the fox said to himself:

"To refrain

Is to gain—

Praise be to Allah that I was so cautious; but let me see what my friend the wolf thinks of this."

So the fox returned home and said to the wolf, "Allah hath made plain for thee a way into the vineyard."

"How should that be?" said the wolf, "how can such a one as thou know such a thing?"

"Why," said the fox, "I went to the vineyard myself. I saw that the owner was dead (torn to pieces by wolves, so they say) and there was the fruit shining amongst the vines."

The wolf doubted not so precise a report as this and his gluttony was aroused and he set off for the vineyard, with the fox not far behind him.

"There," said the fox, directing him to the fallen wall, "thou mayst enter without the trouble of climbing a ladder," and the wolf jumped and fell straight into the pit.

At this the fox sat back on his haunches and laughed with his chops wide open and his tongue hanging out. But before long he heard the wolf in the pit lamenting and crying, so he, too, put on a sad, tearful face and looked over the

side of the hole. "Why, Friend Fox," said the wolf, "I see that thou, too, art saddened by this dismal fate that has befallen me—but can we not devise a means by which I may escape this pit?"

"Nay, nay, Friend Wolf," said the fox, "do not misunderstand me. I do not weep for thy plight, but for all the long life that has passed, when thou demeaned me and smote me; and I weep that thou didst not fall into this pit months ago." And with that the wolf and the fox fell to arguing over their past life together, and eventually it seemed that the wolf repented. "In truth," he said, "I have woefully wronged thee, but if Allah deliver me from this pit I will assuredly reform my ways, take on the mantle of holiness, and go upon the mountains like a pilgrim praising Him."

At these humble words the fox took pity on the wolf and, coming up to the pit, he turned and dangled his tail over the edge so that the wolf might seize it and drag himself out. But no sooner had he done so than the wolf gave one big tug to his tail and pulled him into the pit as well. "So-ho!" he said, "thou fox of little mercy, one minute thou art up there laughing at me, and the next thou art down here once more under my dominion. Assuredly I will hasten to slay thee before thou seest me slain."

"Aha!" said the fox to himself, "now am I indeed fallen back into the snare of the tyrant and I must use all my craft and cunning to escape this foe." And forthwith he began to argue with the wolf, saying that he had offered help only because the wolf had repented and turned to Allah and that it would do his case no good if they both were to die in the pit, but that they might yet both be saved. "If thou stand up at thy full height," he said, "and I climb on thy back so that I come near the top of the hole, then may I spring and reach the ground and fetch the wherewithal to rescue thee."

The wolf placed no trust in this plan, but he perceived that there might be no other way of getting out of the pit, so he permitted the fox to mount his shoulders, raised himself up to his full height, and the fox jumped out of the pit like a chestnut jumping out of the fire. "O double-deceiver," he cried to the wolf, "make sure of thy repentance and call truly to Allah, for I will never trust thee again."

And at that he climbed on the wall overlooking the vineyard and cried to the men working among the vines that a wolf was fallen into the pit. And as all the men came running with sticks and stones to slay the wolf, the fox walked quietly down to the vineyard and ate up all the grapes.

And then Sheherezade went on to tell:—

THE FABLE OF THE MONGOOSE AND THE MOUSE

Once upon a time there lived together in the house of an old farmer a mongoose and a mouse, sharing and sharing whatever food they might come by. Now it so happened that the farmer fell sick and the village doctor ordered that he should be given a diet of sesame seeds with the husks taken off. So the farmer's wife sought a measure of sesame from her neighbours and she steeped it in water, took off the husks and spread it out to dry; then she went about her tasks in the fields.

Well, the mongoose observed these goings-on, which seemed to him like the preparation of a banquet for mongooses, and when the farmer's wife went out he came in and began to carry off the husked sesame to his dwelling behind the wall. He laboured at the work all day, and by the evening, when the farmer's wife came back, she found only a few seeds left on the table.

"By Allah!" she said, "there is a thief at work," and she sat down with a cudgel and watched.

After a time the mongoose came out of his hole to bring in all that remained for his feast. However, he perceived the farmer's wife with her cudgel and he said to himself, "So-ho, this lady may be after taking the skins off more than sesame seeds. It behoves me to be prudent," and he straightway returned to his hole and began to carry forth the seeds that he had already collected and lay them back among the rest.

"Forsooth," said the farmer's wife, "this creature cannot be the cause of our loss for he brings the sesame back from the hole of him who stole it. Kindness must surely be the reward of kindness." And she held her hand and continued to sit and watch.

Now the mongoose guessed what she might be thinking and when he saw his companion the mouse, he said, "O my sister, I should not be a good neighbour to you if I did not tell you that our hosts out there, the farmer and his wife, have brought home a feast of sesame. They have eaten their fill of it, and now there are leavings fit for the king and queen of the mice, strewn all over the table."

So, squeaking for joy, the mouse ran from her hole and frisked and frolicked amongst the grain which the mongoose had so diligently returned to the table.

And when the farmer's wife saw this she deduced that here was the culprit and she smote the mouse with her cudgel, bonk!

From that day forth the mongoose lived a life of ease and contentment, cared for by the farmer's wife and not sharing a morsel with anyone.

[53]

When these fables were told Sheherezade went on to relate to the Shah Shahryar many extravagant stories of the kings and caliphs of Arabia.

There was, for instance:
The Pathetic Tale of Ali bin Bakkar and Shams al-Nahar and their unrequited love;

The Fantastic Tale of Kamar al-Zaman who chose never to wed mortal woman but changed his mind when the spirits of the air brought to him, as though in a dream, the Princess Budur, who had chosen never to wed a mortal man; and

The Strange Tale of Mohammed bin Ali, the jeweller, who pretended to be the Caliph of Baghdad out of frustrated love for the Lady Dunya, the sister of the Caliph's Wazir.

And after such tales as these Sheherezade told:—

THE TALE OF THE EBONY HORSE

His Coming

In times gone by there lived a great and generous Emperor of the Persians and he had one son and three daughters—all as radiant as the full moon. Every year the Emperor was accustomed to hold two festivals, at the time of the New Year and at the Autumn Equinox, when his palace would be open to all who cared to enter and when there would be much rejoicing and giving of gifts. And so it came about that one year three sages came questing to the palace, bringing curious presents by which they hoped to obtain betrothal to the Emperor's three daughters.

The first sage, who was from India, laid before the Emperor the carved figure of a man, inlaid with jewels and bearing a golden trumpet. "What then is the virtue of this gift?" asked the Emperor, and the Indian sage explained that the figure had only to be set up at the gate of the city for it to be guardian over all. "If an enemy approaches," said the sage, "it will blow a blast on this clarion-trumpet and he will be seized of a palsy and drop down dead." So the trumpeter was set up at the gate and the sage was granted the hand of the Emperor's eldest daughter in marriage.

The second sage, who was from Greece, laid before the Emperor a basin of silver in whose midst was fashioned a peacock and twenty-four chicks all of beaten gold. "What then is the virtue of this gift?" asked the Emperor, and the

Grecian sage explained that for every hour that passed of the day or night, the peacock would cry and peck one of its twenty-four chicks and flap its wings, and then at the end of the month it would open its beak so that the new crescent moon could be seen inside. And even as he spoke, an hour struck and the peacock cried and pecked and flapped its wings, so the Emperor was well pleased and granted the sage the hand of his second daughter in marriage.

Then there stepped forward the third sage, who was a Persian necromancer, an old man an hundred years old, with white hair and a face like a cobbler's apron: sunken forehead, mangy eyebrows, red goggle eyes, pendulous lips and a nose like a big black aubergine. His gift to the Emperor was a horse, fashioned full-size out of ebony, inlaid with gold and jewels, and harnessed up with saddle, bridle and stirrups. "What then is the virtue of this gift?" asked the Emperor, and the sage replied that one had only to mount the horse and prepare oneself aright, to be able to fly through the air and cover the space of a year in a single day. So the Emperor thanked the Persian magician and granted him the hand of his youngest daughter in marriage.

Now it so happened that the Emperor's daughters had been hiding behind a curtain to watch all these proceedings and when the youngest daughter perceived who her husband was to be, she fled to her chamber and began weeping and wailing and tearing at her hair and her garments. This racket

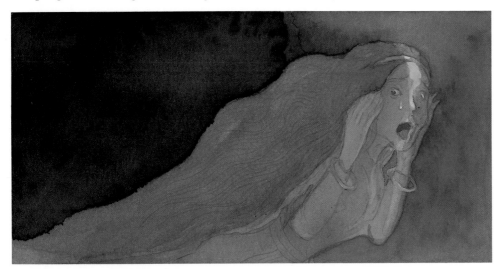

came to the ears of her brother, Kamar al-Akmar, the Moon of Moons, who had just returned from hunting, and he went up to her room and asked her the cause of her distress. "O my brother," she cried, "know that there has come to court this festival day a dreadful magician, with a face like the Jinni who frightens the poultry in the hen-houses; he has given to our father as a gift a horse made of black wood, to which our father has returned him a promise that he may have my hand in marriage. Alas, that I should ever have been born.''

When her brother heard this, he soothed her as best he could and made his way to the Emperor and said, ''Who is this wizard with a face like an ill-made pot who hath bewitched thee into giving away my sister? What is this gift of his that has brought her to such misery?'' So the Emperor told him of the visit of the sages and sent servants to fetch the ebony horse and show it to him, little knowing that the Persian wizard had been standing nearby, had heard everything and was filled with mortification and anger.

So when the servants brought the ebony horse and the Prince mounted it to try its virtues, the sage stepped forward as though to instruct him. ''Trill this,'' he said, pointing to a pin on the side of the horse's head, and the Prince had no sooner turned it than the ebony horse seemed to take breath and soared off into the air, with the Prince sitting astride its back.

''Very well,'' said the Emperor, ''but tell me, O sage, how may he turn the horse and how make it descend?''

''Alas, my lord,'' said the sage, ''I can do nothing, and we may never see him again till Resurrection-day, for he was so proud and eager to be off that he did not stay to ask me what mechanism he might use to bring the creature back to the ground.'' And the magician smiled grimly, for he had so contrived it to be revenged upon the Prince for seeking to thwart his marriage. But the Emperor was himself angry and he ordered that the sorcerer be at once clapped into jail and there bastinadoed on the soles of his feet.

What Happened to the Prince

When he felt the ebony horse move under him and then rise in the air, the Prince was filled with great joy. Never in his years of hunting had he travelled so fast or seen so far as now. But as the horse made unswervingly towards the sun the Prince became troubled in his mind as to how he might turn the beast round, let alone bring it down. ''Verily,'' he said to himself, ''this is a device of the sage to destroy me for championing my sister.''

For a huntsman, though, he was not without wit, and he fell to examining the carcass of his horse in the belief that one pin for setting off might be matched by another pin for setting down and, behold! beneath the carved shoulders of the horse he found what seemed to be two ornamental cocks' heads, and as he twisted one, so he was able to steer the horse and as he twisted the other, so he was able to bring it into a gradual descent. Thus he passed over mountains and deserts, oceans and forests, even to the boundaries of China.

By this time the day was waning and he determined to find somewhere he might pass the night, and he saw below him a fine city with, in its centre, the towers and battlements of a majestic castle. "This is a goodly place," he said to himself, and he turned the pin to descend and the horse sank down with him like a weary bird and alighted gently on the terrace roof of the castle:

"Alhamdohlillah," said the Prince, "praise be to Allah for my safe journeying," and since, by now, the night had fallen he set off through the sleeping palace to see if he might find food and water for himself. First he came to a staircase which took him down to a court paved with white marble and alabaster, shining in the light of the moon; then he traversed chambers and passage-ways, all unguarded and empty, until eventually he came upon the entrance to the harem, at whose door slept a giant eunuch as though he were a tribesman of the Jinn, longer than lumber and broader than a bench. Beside him was his sword, whose pommel gleamed in the candle flames, and above his head on a column of granite there hung a leather bag.

Praying again to Allah, the Prince carefully lifted down the bag and found within it a great store of provisions with which he refreshed himself. He then replaced the bag and, taking the eunuch's sword, he crept forward to where Destiny should take him.

Beyond the door of the harem there was a second door, with a curtain
before it. This he raised and beyond it he saw a couch of white ivory, inlaid with
pearls. Slave girls were sleeping at its corners and upon the couch itself there
slept a lady, beautiful as the moon, and robed only in her hair. The Prince was
overcome by her loveliness and, caring nothing for discovery or death, he
went up to her and kissed her on the cheek. At once she awoke, opened her
eyes and said, "Who art thou and whence camest thou?" to which the Prince
replied, "I am thy slave and thy lover."

"But who brought thee hither?"

"My Lord and my fortune."

Now it so happened that only the day before, the lady's father, who was
King of that land, had had audience of the King of Hind who sought to marry
her; but the King of Hind was ugly and uncouth and had been sent away, but
the lady believed that our Prince was he and she deemed it most blameworthy
that she should be denied one so handsome. So she set about shouting with
anguish, at which her slave girls all woke up and before long the palace was in
uproar. The slave girls woke up the eunuch; the eunuch, missing his sword,
believed that bandits had come to the palace and rushed to wake the King; the
King called up his household guard and everyone ran pell-mell to the
Princess's bedroom, where she continued to wail that she had been cheated
of her lover, and where the Prince Kamar al-Akmar was lost in wonder at
all the hubbub.

Eventually the eunuch explained to the King that he thought vandals had stolen his sword, and the slave girls explained to the eunuch that he had allowed a man to enter the harem, and the Princess explained to the slave girls that she wanted to marry the Prince, whether he came from Hind or no, and the Prince politely said to all and sundry that he would be glad to sign the marriage-contract as soon as it was indited.

None of this could assuage the wrath of the King, though, who did not care for strangers to make themselves so free with his daughter before ever he had been introduced. "How can we know," he cried, "that thou art an Emperor's son as thou sayst? What Emperor shall save thee if I call upon my slaves and servants to put thee to the vilest of deaths?" To which the Prince replied that he would be pleased to stand in single combat for his honour against the King himself or else stand against the King's whole army to gain his daughter's hand.

Well, the King had no liking for single combat against one so doughty as this strange prince, so it was agreed that next morning he should confront the King's whole army, and that was forty thousand horsemen and a like number of slaves and followers. "This Prince, for his honour," cried the King when all were assembled, "this Prince pretendeth that he can overcome you in combat to gain the hand of my daughter and that, were you an hundred thousand, he would force you to flight, so when he comes upon you, show him that he has chosen a mighty task." Then, turning to the Prince, he said, "Up, my son, and slaughter my army."

But the Prince turned to the King and said, "My Lord, how shall I come against this host without any horse?" To which the King gave answer that he might choose any mount from the King's own stables. "But not one of those horses pleaseth me," said the Prince, "I will ride none other but the horse on which I came."

"Then where is thy horse?" asked the King.

"Atop thy palace," answered the Prince.

"Where in my palace?" asked the King.

"On the roof," answered the Prince—and with those words it seemed to the King that this comely, daring fellow was indeed mad.

"How can a horse be on the roof!" he cried; but he forthwith sent servants back to the palace with instructions to bring back whatever they might find on the roof and before long they returned bearing the ebony horse, which, gallant as it looked (and though it was indeed on the roof), hardly seemed a fit charger to accost the King's whole army. "Is this then thy horse?" asked the King.

"Yes, O King, this is my horse; and if thou wilt bid thy troops retire a bowshot from it then I will mount and charge."

So the troops withdrew and the Prince climbed into the saddle and forthwith trilled the pin of ascent; and as everyone watched to see him charge, the horse began to rock and sway as though it were taking great breaths, and then it rose in the air and flew off over the heads of the waiting troops. "Catch him! Catch him!" cried the King; but his Wazirs and ministers replied, "Oh who can overtake a flying bird?" and as the Prince fled away in the sky, the army was left to return to quarters and the King's daughter relapsed into tears and grief.

"By Allah!" she cried, "I will neither eat nor drink nor sleep till Allah return him to me."

The Homecoming of the Ebony Horse

Once the Prince had contrived his flight from the King he set his horse's head in the direction of his homeland and before nightfall he was again in the palace of his father. But how changed everything was. For now, instead of the bright traffic of the festival day, all was still and shrouded, with black hangings on the walls and ashes strewn upon the floor; and when he made his way to the Emperor's chamber he found his father and mother and his sisters clad in the black robes of mourning and pale with grief.

When he entered the room though, they started up in surprise for it was his supposed death that they had been mourning, and before long they were clambering over him, hugging and kissing him and shouting for joy. The Emperor ordered a great banquet to be prepared and a holiday was proclaimed throughout the land. Streets and markets were hung with garlands, drums and cymbals were beaten, and a general pardon was given to all who were imprisoned (including, not least, the Persian necromancer, who was rewarded with robes and honour now that the ebony horse had returned, but of whose marriage to the King's youngest daughter nothing more was said).

Amid all the merriment, however, the Prince felt little but sadness and longing for the Princess that he had left behind so far away. He confessed his love to his father, the Emperor, saying that he was determined once more to mount his ebony horse and ride to find her, and his father gave his consent—although privately he wished to make nothing more than a bonfire of the horse and its tricks.

So the Prince rode once more into the sky and made his way to that palace roof where he had alighted so few days ago. He made his way quietly to the harem, finding the eunuch asleep as usual; but when he came to the Princess's chamber there was little need for quietness since she was still wailing and bawling over the loss of the Prince who had flown away. As soon as she saw

him, however, she was struck dumb with wonder, and when he suggested that she might this time ride back with him to his father's kingdom she was overwhelmed with joy. She dressed herself in the richest of her dresses, furnished herself with all manner of gold ornaments and jewels, and the Prince then carried her up to the terrace roof where the ebony horse patiently waited. They climbed on its back and the Prince secured the Princess to him with bonds of silk, twisted the pin to ascend and away they flew over forests and oceans, deserts and mountains, back to the land of Persia.

When the city of the Emperor came in sight, the Prince determined that he would take his bride to one of the pavilions in the Emperor's garden where she might rest awhile, before he summoned his father and the royal court to greet her. Accordingly, he caused the horse to alight in a secluded corner of the grounds and there he left the Princess, seated in a summer-house, while he went to announce their arrival. "Rest here," he said, "and watch over our horse, until I, or my messenger, come to thee to bring thee an Emperor's welcome to this land," and he forthwith betook himself to the palace to give tidings of their coming to his father and his family.

[65]

Great was the joy at his return. The Emperor straightway ordered a continuance of the general rejoicing and prepared a great train of courtiers and ministers, members of the royal household, slaves and eunuchs to go to make welcome the Princess. He himself led the procession and to the music of drums and trumpets they made their way across the gardens to the summer-house.

But when they arrived, they discovered with dismay and consternation that no one was there. The Princess and the ebony horse had gone.

What Happened to the Princess

Now it so chanced that when the Prince brought the ebony horse to rest in his father's demesne he was observed by the Persian necromancer who was in the garden seeking herbs and simples for his cauldron. With great caution, therefore, he slunk over to the pavilion and overheard the last of the Prince's conversation with his bride.

Allowing a suitable amount of time to elapse, the wizard then made his way to the Princess, bowed down before her and kissed the ground between his hands. "And who art thou?" asked the Princess, not a little alarmed at the sudden appearance of a man of such monstrous ugliness.

"O my lady," said the wizard, "I come from the Prince, who hath bidden me to conduct thee to the palace of his father."

"Why came he not himself? And could he not find a messenger more handsome for this joyous occasion?"

"Ah, my lady," said the wizard, "he is even now preparing a royal greeting for thee; while as to myself, is it not fitting that so bright a jewel as thou art, should be set off against so plain an attendant as I?"

"Very well," she said, "then let us go forward to the Prince. But what hast thou brought for me to ride?"

"O my lady, thou mayst ride the horse that thou camest on."

"But I cannot ride it myself."

"Then I must needs accompany thee," said the magician, and he mounted the ebony horse, took the Princess up behind him, and after binding her securely in her seat he trilled the ascent-pin and the horse gathered itself and rose into the air. Away it went, beyond the confines of the palace, beyond the city—over the hills and far away.

"Ho thou," cried the Princess, "where goest thou? Where is the Prince?"

"Allah damn the Prince," cried the magician, "he is a mean, skinflint knave!"

"Then woe to thee, that thou disobeyest thy Lord's commandment!"

"He is no Lord of mine, but rather my enemy. For thou must know that I am the creator and master of this horse, which he took from me by a stratagem, and now that I have it again I shall never relinquish it. Thou and I shall fare forward into a new life of power and riches." And he turned the horse's head towards the west and ceased not to ride till they reached the land of the Greeks where he brought them all to rest in a green meadow by a stream.

Now this meadow lay close to the city of a great Grecian king, who at that time was walking nearby in the cool of the evening. When he saw this strange pair with their wooden horse, the rough-visaged Persian and the comely lady, he deemed some mystery was afoot and he sent his slaves to take them and bring them to audience at his royal palace.

"Who art thou?" he asked, "and whence comest thou with thy toy horse?"

"We are of Persia," said the magician, "way-worn travellers, man and wife." But the lady would not hear of such a thing. "O King," she cried, "that is not so. He is naught but a wicked necromancer who has stolen me away by force and fraud . . ." and she prostrated herself before the King.

Well, there seemed little doubt as to the truth of her denunciations, and the Grecian king ordered the sage to be taken to prison and there (again) bastinadoed. The mysterious horse he placed within his treasure-house, and the lady within his harem where she fell to weeping and wailing so that none could come near her.

[67]

And How it All Ended

Now when the Prince Kamar al-Akmar discovered the summer-house empty in the garden, with horse and Princess gone, he realized that their disappearance could only be the work of the Persian necromancer, for he alone knew the secret mechanisms of the horse's flight. So the Prince bade farewell to his father and his family and set out into the world to find the villain.

He travelled through many lands, inquiring if people had heard tell of a strange horse of ebony that flew down out of the sky—but apart from suggestions made about the state of his own wits he was told nothing. Then one day, arriving at a certain khan, he came upon some merchants talking and overheard one of them tell how in such-and-such a city in Greece the King had come upon an ill-assorted couple—a foul-visaged Persian and a beautiful maiden—standing beside a wooden horse which they seemed to have carried to the middle of a field but could carry no further.

At once the Prince besought the merchant for a closer account of what he had heard, and when he had ascertained the name and region of the city he turned his steps towards that part of Greece and did not rest until he was outside its walls. When he arrived, though, it was evening and he was taken into the gatehouse to be questioned and to be held for the night. "Where are you from?" they asked.

"I am a Persian from Persia," he replied, at which the guardsmen fell back with laughter (for in those days the Persians were deemed great liars and the Greeks had a joke about one of them who said, "I am a Persian, but I am not lying now"). "Ho, ho," said the guard, "well let's hope that that is not so great a lie as the ones we have been hearing from that other Persian traveller who even now is taking his ease in our prison." And he went on to tell the story of the King's discovery of the magician and the Princess, how the one kept speaking of a horse that flew through the air and how the other was in a fit of madness, wailing and raving, so that never a doctor could get near to cure her—for the King had fallen madly in love with her and was seeking physicians from all quarters of the earth who might mend her wits.

From these words the Prince gained some notion of how he might proceed in his plan to rescue the Princess, and the next morning, when he was brought before the King, he put out that he was a travelling doctor come to try to cure the Princess's madness. So the King had him taken to the chamber where the Princess was kept and there he found her, not possessed of any evil Jinn, but writhing and wringing her hands that none might approach her.

When the Prince saw her thus he bade her attendants leave the room and he stepped towards her saying, "No harm shall betide thee, O ravishment of the

three worlds''; and when she perceived who spoke she fell down as though in a swoon. Then the Prince went up to her and whispered to her to be calm and patient. She was now to pretend to be cured and was to speak kindly to the King who sought her love, and if Allah willed then they would reach an end of their tribulations.

Then the Prince returned to the King and bade him go in to the woman, for he had taken away her madness. ''But beware,'' he said, ''for the completion of her cure it behoveth that thou go forth with all thy guards to the place where thou foundest her, nor shouldst thou forget the beast of black wood which was with her. Therein lies a devil and unless I exorcise him he will return to her and afflict her again.''

So the King did as this physician asked. He visited the Princess and was filled with joy at the sweetness of her recovery and he bade his servants bathe her and dress her royally in fine robes and jewels. Then he and the Princess and all the army moved out to the field where first he had seen her and there on the sward they had set up the ebony horse.

''My lord the King,'' said the Prince, ''with thy leave and at thy word I will now proceed to fumigations and conjurations, that we may drive the evil spirit from this horse; but I must first place the damsel upon its back that we may observe whether or no there be a conjunction of spirits.'' And so, placing the Princess on the horse's back, he jumped into the saddle and urging her to cling to him tightly, he trilled the pin of ascent. The horse shuddered again as though it were drawing breath and forthwith rode up out of the field and over the heads of the King and his army and away across the seas to Persia.

Then was the marriage of the Princess to Prince Kamar al-Akmar indeed celebrated and messages of joy and consolation were despatched to the Princess's father that he might know of his daughter's happiness. As for the Persian magician, for all we know he continued to elaborate his spells in the Greek King's prison till the end of his days, and as for the ebony horse, the Emperor gained his wish and it was burned on a bonfire on the Prince's wedding-night.

 When this Tale of the Ebony Horse was finished, Dunyazad pleaded with Sheherezade to tell the Sultan the jests she knew of the pride and foolishness of men, and amongst a score of stories there was none that pleased the Shah Shahryar more than:—

THE TALE WHICH ALI THE PERSIAN TOLD
TO AMUSE HARUN AL-RASHID

Know thou, O Commander of the Faithful (said the Persian to Harun), that some years ago I took it into my head to leave Baghdad, and go a-travelling; and I had with me a boy who carried my leather bag.

Now one day, as we were passing through a certain city, a rascally Kurdish man fell upon us, seized the bag and cried out that we had stolen it from him. "How can that be," I said, "seeing that I have brought it with me from Baghdad?" But he would not believe me and there was nothing for it but we must take the matter before the magistrate.

"What brings you here and what is your quarrel?" asked the justice.

"Allah preserve your lordship," said the Kurdish man, "but this Persian vagabond claims to have brought that bag from Baghdad, but the bag is in truth no Baghdad bag at all but my bag, bagging up all my rightful belongings."

"When did you lose it?" asked the justice.

"But yesterday," said the Kurd.

"Well, if it's yours," said the justice, "tell me what is in it."

"Why," said the Kurd, "that bag contains:

two silver brushes for eye-powder and antimony for the eyes,
a handkerchief, wrapping up two gilt cups and two candlesticks,

two tents with two plates, two spoons and a cushion,

two leather rugs, two jugs and a brass tray,

[73]

two basins, two water-jars and a pot with a ladle,

two sacks, two saddles and a needle,

two sheep, two lambs and a she-goat,

two dogs, two bitches and a she-cat,

two green pavilions with a camel and two she-camels,

a lioness, two lions and a she-bear,

two jackals and a mattress,

two sofas and an upper-chamber,

two saloons and a portico, and a whole company of Kurds who will bear
witness that this
bag is my bag.''

Then the judge turned to me and said, ''Well, sir, and what do you say?''
So I came forward in great bewilderment and said:
''Allah preserve your lordship, but in truth there is nothing in this bag save:

a little ruined tenement and a dog-house,

a boys' school with the boys playing dice,

and several tents and tent-ropes,

and an ironsmith's forge and a fishing-net,

and the cities of Baghdad and Basra, with the palace of Shaddad-bin-Ad and a thousand citizens who will bear witness that this is my bag."

So when he heard this the Kurdish man wept and wailed and cried again a great long list of all the things that were in the bag, to which I could only reply with a list of equal length.

"Well, then," said the justice, "I can see that you two are little more than pestilential fellows, come to waste the time of all learned judges and magistrates. Never yet, from China to Shajarat Umm Ghaylan, or from Persia to Sudan, or from Wadi Nu'uman to Khorasan, did I hear of a bag so bottomless as this." And he bade his servants open the bag . . . and there was inside it:

a knob of cheese,   a lemon   and two olives.

So I gave the bag to the Kurdish man and went my way.

 And when Sheherezade had told this tale which Ali the Persian had told to the Caliph Harun al-Rashid, she went on to relate little stories of the generosity of the Caliph and of his Wazir, Ja'afer, and she also told the story of:—

MA'AN BIN-ZAIDAH, THE DONKEY AND THE CUCUMBERS

Now the Emir Ma'an bin-Zaidah was a man of great wealth and generosity. One day he was out hunting and came upon a herd of gazelles which he and his men pursued, each one to a different point of the compass. And Ma'an ran down the gazelle that he was chasing and slaughtered it, and while he was cutting and dressing it he saw an old man riding out of the desert on a donkey.

"Greetings," said Ma'an, "and where do you come from on that handsome donkey?"

"My lord," said the old man, "I am from Kuza'ah—a poor outpost in the desert where it is all we can do from one year to the next to raise a few beans. But this year has been a season of plenty and I have raised a fine crop of curly cucumbers which I am carrying to the Emir Ma'an bin-Zaidah, for it is well known that he is a lord of boundless generosity."

"Well," said Ma'an, "and how much do you hope to get from Ma'an bin-Zaidah for this handsome and succulent crop of curly cucumbers?"

"Why," said the old man, "surely a thousand dinars."

"A thousand dinars, eh?" said Ma'an bin-Zaidah, "and what if he says that that is too much?"

"Why then," said the old man, "five hundred."

"And what if he says that that is too much?"

"Why then, three hundred."

And so it went on, with the old man cutting the price from three hundred, to two hundred, to one hundred, to fifty, to thirty . . .

"And what if he says that that is too much?" asked Ma'an.

"Well," said the old man, "I will give him this handsome donkey and these succulent curly cucumbers and I will go home with nothing."

And so they parted, and Ma'an met up again with his company and returned to his palace where he bathed and dressed himself in his robes and sat in his chair of state surrounded by his slaves and his eunuchs and all his other attendants.

Along came the old man with his donkey and his panniers.

"Greetings," said Ma'an bin-Zaidah, "what brings you here, old man of the desert?"

"My lord," said the old man, who could not recognize Ma'an bin-Zaidah amid the trappings of his court, "I come to honour the Emir and to bring him a bounty of curly cucumbers."

"And how much do you want for these curly cucumbers?"

"Why, my lord, surely a thousand dinars."

"Impossible! that is far too much."

"Why, then, my lord, five hundred."

"Scandalous! that is far too much."

"Why, then, my lord, three hundred . . ."

And so they bargained, from three hundred, to two hundred, to one hundred, to fifty, to thirty with Ma'an bin-Zaidah saying all the time, "but that is far too much."

"By Allah," cried the old man, "my meeting in the desert was unlucky and ill-omened, but I will not take less than thirty dinars.''

And then Ma'an bin-Zaidah laughed and the old man recognized him for the hunter in the desert, and he said, ''Ah, my lord, if you will not give me the thirty dinars then there is my donkey tied to your door-post.''

And Ma'an laughed again and said, ''Give him his thousand dinars, and his five hundred, and his three hundred, and his two hundred, and his one hundred, and his fifty and his thirty—but leave me the donkey at the door-post! I must have the donkey!''

And the old man returned to Kuza'ah rejoicing, loaded down with two thousand, one hundred and eighty dinars, but with never a beast to carry him home.

 At the end of the story of the cucumbers, the night was still dark over the Shah Shahryar's palace and so Dunyazad called upon her sister Sheherezade to tell them:–

THE STORY OF SINDBAD THE PORTER
AND SINDBAD THE SAILOR

In the days when Harun al-Rashid was Caliph in Baghdad there dwelt in that city a poor man who was known as Sindbad the Porter, for he made what living he could by carrying baggage on his head for hire.

One day, when the sun was at its hottest and his burden at its heaviest, he found himself beside the gate of a merchant's house. The courtyard beyond the gate was fresh with full-scented flowers, and from the rooms of the house there came the sounds of lutes and zithers and voices more beautiful than song-birds. "Truly, there is no God but Allah," said Sindbad the Porter, "and whom He wishes to raise He exalts and whom He wishes to abase He makes low," and, raising his voice he sang the verses:

> "Thou, Ruler of Heaven, hast placed the rich man
> There in his castle; the poor man at his gate.
> Thou, Ruler of Heaven, teach us Thy patience
> That we rejoice in Thee, whatever be our fate."

Now it so happened that the master of the house was walking in a room overlooking the street where Sindbad was singing, and he forthwith sent a servant to bring the porter before him. Thus it came about that he was led through rooms hung with fine tapestries and adorned with rich furnishings into the presence of the master: a man, grey with age but of resplendent

nobility, sitting among a company of lords at tables garnished with meat and fruits and bowls of wine. Slave girls were playing instruments and singing and it seemed to the porter that he had entered Paradise.

"Welcome," said the master of the house; and he called for food and drink to be placed before his new guest, who, in wonderment, gave praise to Allah, washed his hands, and set to eating as though there might be no more tomorrows in his life. When he had finished the master of the house welcomed him again and asked to know his name and calling.

"My name is Sindbad the Porter," said the man, "and I make my living by carrying other people's goods about the town for hire."

"Now that is passing strange," said the lord, "for my name too is Sindbad—although men call me Sindbad the Sailor—and I too have carried burdens on my back in my time. And when I heard you singing outside my house of the virtues of patience, it brought back to my mind the trials that I too have undergone, and it seemed to me a worthy act that I might offer you my hospitality and set before you the proof that suffering may lead to good cheer, and the way to prosperity may lie through hardship and privation."

 And—as if she had been present at this banquet—Sheherezade began to tell Shah Shahryar of the Seven Voyages of Sindbad the Sailor just as he had told them to the Porter, his namesake.

THE TALE OF THE VANISHING ISLAND

I should have known from the start (he said) that my engaging to be a mariner was going to be a courtship with calamity. Indeed, if I had behaved myself, I need never have gone to sea at all, for I was born of a wealthy father and only reduced myself to the poverty of one like yourself, O Sindbad the Porter, by too much lavish eating and drinking and by giving myself unrestrained to the delights of youth. So it came about that I had to gather up what remnants of wealth that I had and travel forth with them to trade in different quarters of the world from the Pillars of Hercules in the west to Serendib in the east.

We had not sailed long on my very first voyage before we came to an island that seemed like a little corner of Paradise. Trees and flowers blossomed on its fine soil and birds and small game were there for our eating. Accordingly we cast anchor and landed, and while some went to catch a fresh dinner for us, others set to lighting great fires for the cooking. Imagine our amazement, therefore, when the ship's master suddenly blew warnings to us on his clarion and summoned us back to the vessel. For this was no island at all that we had camped on, but a huge fish who had lain so long on the surface of the ocean that dust and sand had gathered on his back and nourished the undergrowth through which we hunted. Now the heat from our cooking-fires was so disturbing him that he grew uneasy. With a few quivers, like the first tremors of an earthquake, he flexed the muscles of his back and then suddenly he dived for the cool depths of the sea, leaving those of us who had not got back to the ship floating in an atoll of uprooted trees and bushes.

Only with the utmost difficulty did I escape from this wreckage of my fortune, and only by strange coincidence did I find again the goods and gear that I had left on board the ship; but I did not let this narrow encounter deter me from further voyaging, which led to:–

THE ADVENTURE OF THE VALLEY OF DIAMONDS

I had taken ship, once more to go trading, and again we hove to at an island (but this time surely too large and mountainous to be a sleeping fish). While my fellows set about exploring and bringing aboard fresh water, I wandered off on my own to enjoy what I could find of the fruits of the island and to offer prayers and praises to the Omnipotent King.

Later I rested beneath a tree, where I fell asleep, and when I woke it was to find myself alone, for my companions had forgotten me and had sailed without me. Not knowing what to do, I set out to search the shore for help, but could find no trace of human habitation.

On climbing a tree, however, the better to see what lay inland, I observed, glinting in the sunshine, a huge white dome beyond the far side of a forest. So, with great difficulty, I made my way in that direction and eventually arrived at what seemed to be a strange building. It was smooth and pale as alabaster, with its walls curving up to meet the sky, but with no sign of doors or windows through which I might enter.

I set off to walk round it, and I had not gone fifty paces before the day darkened as though the sun had suddenly swept down below the horizon. As I peered westwards though, I saw that I had not been overtaken by a magic sunset, but that a gigantic bird was flying towards me, whose mighty body and widespread wings were hiding the sun from sight.

And in the darkness all suddenly became clear to me. For I remembered seamen's tales of a huge bird called a Rukh that was wont to lay eggs as big as a castle and that fed its young upon elephants. Surely this was just such an one, and surely the dome round which I was walking was none other than the Rukh's egg.

So it proved. The bird circled slowly out of the sun and came to rest on the surface of the dome, covering the shell with its breast and trailing its legs behind, towards the forest; and thus it fell asleep. As it slept though, I bethought me that this might prove an apt means for my escape, and I unwound my turban from my head, twisted it into a rope, and secured myself with it to one of the legs of the Rukh.

There I lay during the night, and in the morning the bird gave a great cry and rose from its nest on its mighty wings and flew with me over the ocean towards land. Eventually it came to rest on top of a high hill and here I speedily untied myself and watched as the bird took off again and swooped on some invisible object in the valley below. As it mounted towards heaven again though, I perceived that it held in its talons a monstrous wriggling serpent that it had plucked from the side of the hill, and as I followed the course that it had taken, I saw that I was lodged in a desert region of rocks and mountains, far less hospitable than the island from which I had flown.

Nevertheless, in search of water, I made my way towards the valley-bottom and discovered as I went that the whole place swarmed with snakes and serpents, each as big as a palm tree. It seemed that they spent much of the day

hiding in holes and caves for fear of being attacked by the Rukhs, and all around their lairs, and spread across the valley floor, there glinted what looked like a pavement of glass. As I got nearer though, I saw that this was a delusion and that the ground was really scattered with diamonds, which lay as thick as the sands by the sea.

As I stood marvelling at all this wealth, lying amongst the serpents, I heard a strange bumping sound and I saw tumbling down the hill towards me a huge piece of meat, as it were the side of an ox; and as it fell, all sticky and bloody as it was, so it gathered to its surface the loose diamonds among which it was rolling. Then I remembered that I had heard tell of the stratagems of diamond-hunters, who proceeded in this way, tossing raw meat amongst the precious stones so that it might be lifted out of the valley by carnivorous birds from whom the diamonds could then be collected.

Trusting to this knowledge, I filled my pockets and my girdle and my turban with as many diamonds as I could and seized hold of the underside of the carcase, all raw and bloody as it was, and awaited events. Sure enough, before long, a great eagle swooped out of the sky and seized the meat in his talons and lifted it—and me—high out of the valley and brought us to ground by its nest on the other side of the mountain. In only a few moments, however, after our landing, there started a great racket of shouting and banging of gongs and from out of hiding came a group of diamond-hunters intent on holding the eagle at bay till they should pluck out whatever riches might be stuck to his dinner.

They were not a little amazed to find a man also entangled with the carcase, but when I told them my adventures and shared with them the stones that I had brought up from the valley, they wished that they might have such surprises every day. And so we returned to their camp and ate and drank until we all cried for Rukhs to come and carry us home.

As it happened though (said Sindbad to Sindbad), this was not the last of my encounters with the Rukh. For after several more years and several more voyages that bird became the direct cause of my adventure with:−

THE OLD MAN OF THE SEA

I had set sail from Basra with a goodly company, and after several weeks voyaging we found ourselves once again on an island where the Rukhs had chosen to nest. I did not know this when we landed, nor had I ever told my shipmates of my own discovery of the egg, so when some of them saw the white dome rising above the tree-line they had no notion of the dangers that it might portend.

Several of them made their way to examine the object and when (like me) they could find no sign on its smooth walls of what it might be, they began banging it with stones and beating it with fallen branches until suddenly, as all eggs will, it cracked open and they were like to be drowned in the watery fluid that streamed out over them.

As the flood subsided though, they perceived within the egg the body of the young Rukh and forthwith pulled it out and brought it back to the ship to be a handsome augmentation of our stores. But when I heard their story and recognized what they had done, I went straightway to the ship's master and urged him to set sail without delay. "Vengeance will be upon us otherwise," I said.

And I was right. For although the master called his men aboard and stood off from the island as fast as he could, it was not long before the sun was darkened by the wings of the returning birds. When they discovered the destruction wrought upon their egg, they began to utter piercing cries and rose vertically into the air to see who might have done such a thing. Nor did it take even their bird-brains long to determine that we were the culprits and we had barely got a league or two clear of the island before they appeared above us, each carrying in its claws a massive boulder brought from the tops of the mountains.

As soon as the he-Rukh came up with us, he let fall his rock from a great height. But the ship's master saw it coming and put the ship about so that the rock plunged into the sea—but with such violence that we were pitched high on the crest of the wave it made and looked down into the trough to see the bottom of the ocean laid momentarily bare. Then the she-Rukh let fall her boulder, which was bigger than that of her mate, and, as Destiny decreed, it fell straight on to the poop of our ship so that the vessel burst asunder in a thousand pieces and we were all cast into the sea.

Such was the tumult of the waves after this battering that there was no hope of us staying together, and before long I found myself separated from my companions and drifting aimlessly astride one of the planks of the broken ship. Through the intercession of Allah, however, I was eventually able to paddle my way towards the shore-line of an unknown coast and there I landed, yearning for food and water to refresh myself.

As I began to explore this new land, however, so it seemed to me that the Divine One had brought me to the edge of His Demesne. For here were fruits and flowers in abundance and clear streams, running with purest water, and all I had to do was to gather and drink my fill to be restored to life. So there I stayed till nightfall, hearing no voice and seeing no other man, and after giving thanks to the Most High and glorifying Him, I lay down and slept till morning.

Next day, following a stream in search of human habitations, I came upon a deep spring, flowing from a well, and there, beside the well, sat a venerable old man dressed in a skirt of palm fronds. I greeted him and he returned my salaam, but never a word he spoke. "Then tell me, nuncle," I said, "why do you sit silent here?" Again he bowed towards me and groaned, signalling with his hand as if to say that he wished to cross the channel from the well but could not do so. So I knelt down, that he might climb on my shoulders, and I stepped into the water and carried him to where he had pointed.

When we reached the other side, I stooped so that he might dismount, but as I did so he wound his legs more tightly round my neck and made no move to be gone. And when I looked at his legs and saw them black and rough like a buffalo's hide I took fright and sought to throw him from me, but to no avail. He clung to me and gripped my neck with his legs till I was nearly choked, and though I fell to the ground and writhed with the pain of it, still he stayed with me. Then he drummed his heels upon me and beat my back with his arms, which were like palm rods, and there was nothing I could do but rise and carry him where it seemed he wanted to go.

From that day forth he stayed as though pinioned upon my back. He drove me among the trees so that he might reach for the sweetest fruits, he lived and slept upon me as though I were there for his domestic comfort, and if ever I refused to do his bidding or loitered about too slowly he would bang me with his arms and feet, so that I was driven nearly mad.

"What reward is this for compassion?" I cried. "By Allah, if I live beyond this time I shall never more do any man service." And so in weariness I wandered on until one day we came to a place where there was an abundance of gourds fallen from their trees and drying in the sun. So I took a large dry gourd, cut it open, and hollowed it out and cleaned it. Then I gathered grapes

which grew on a vine nearby and squeezed them into the gourd till it was full of their juice, and I stopped up its mouth and left it in the sun that it might ferment and become strong wine. In this way I brewed a potion to sustain me through my troubles and bring me some measure of cheerfulness.

One day, as I was unstoppering one of my gourds of wine, the Old Man on my back signed to me that he wished to know what I was drinking. "Ha ha!" I cried, "it is such liquor as makes even porters happy," and I began to dance and reel among the trees with the old man jogging on my shoulders. When he realized how frolicsome the wine appeared to make me, he began drumming on my head and gurgling as much as to say that he, too, wanted a portion. So I passed up a gourd full of the fermented brew and he drained it to the dregs and hurled it into the forest and at once began jigging up and down, mouthing strange noises, which I took to be his kind of singing:

> "yorhorlorlorlor,
>   yorhorlorlorlor,
>   yorhorlorlorlorkus
>   yorhorlorlorlor!"

And as the fumes of the wine rolled round his brain so his side-muscles and his limbs relaxed and I was at last able to tip him off my shoulders on to the ground—yorhorlorlorlor!

There he lay, out of his senses with drunkenness. So I went among the trees and found a great stone and smote him on the head with it, that he might never more be a curse to travellers. Then I took my way back to the sea-coast and dwelt in peace, tending my sores, until I saw the sail of a passing ship and was able to signal to it to put in and rescue me.

When the sailors questioned me as to who I was and how I came to be stranded on this coast, they marvelled to hear of my adventure with the creature that tormented me. "For you should know," they said, "that he is spoken of in these parts as Sheikh a-Bahr, which is to say the Old Man of the Sea, and none but you has ever borne that burden and survived. For those that he traps he marches till they die under him, and then he eats them . . ."

So (said Sindbad the Sailor to Sindbad the Porter), thus may you see how I have done my share of carrying in the world, but such has been my patience under oppression and my perseverance through so many voyages that I came to safe harbour here at last—and since the days are long gone since I swore never to show compassion, and since thou art well-met as a man of my name, let us render praise to Allah that we live in a world so full of His mercies that we shall all at last come safe to shore.

And Sindbad the Sailor and Sindbad the Porter drank and made merry and were as brothers from that day forth.

"So those were some of the strange adventures of Sindbad the Sailor," said Sheherezade to the Shah Shahryar, "but none was so strange as what I would now tell you of:–

THE TALE OF THE CITY OF BRASS

Of the Jars of Solomon

Many nights ago (said Sheherezade to the Shah Shahryar) and many stories past, we heard tell of that fisherman who brought up from the depths of the ocean a jar, sealed with the seal of Solomon the King; and you will recall that therein was imprisoned a prince of the Jann upon whom the anger of King Solomon had fallen.

Now it so happens that, in days of ancient time, there dwelt in the city of Damascus a Caliph by the name of Abd al-Malik bin Marwan who loved nothing better than to gather about him his sultans and his grandees to hear tidings of the wide world beyond his own domain. Well, one day there came to him a courtier, one Talib bin Sahl, who was renowned as a man of great learning, even though his study was always to the end of uncovering deep secrets of those places in the world where treasures might be hid.

"Commander of the Faithful," said Talib, "there has come to me news of a strange voyage that was undertaken once by my grandfather who recounted his adventures to my father, through whom they have come down to me." And Talib went on to describe how his grandfather had been carried by storms beyond the great island of Sicily and had made landfall in an unknown country of desert and mountains whose people had no knowledge of the Goodness and Mercy of Allah the Most High. Nevertheless, when the sea-folk of that land went fishing they would often draw up in their nets just such brass jars as those we heard tell of, stamped with the signet of Solomon; and whenever they unstoppered such jars out would come the twisting black smoke of the Jinni, forming itself into a giant whose head was higher than the mountain tops and who would vanish into the empyrean crying: "I repent, I repent; pardon me O prophet of Allah!" (for the Jinni knew not that Solomon had been dead time out of mind).

The Caliph Abd al-Malik marvelled at Talib's story, for he knew the runes of the All-wise:

'Rise Solomon, and rule Our Land in strength and majesty,
And those who honour not Our Name, subdue for all eternity';

and it came to him that he would like to look upon these brass jars, that they might be a lesson to those who would learn and a warning to those who would be warned. So he consulted with Talib how this might be, and Talib prepared for him a plan whereby a journey might be made under truce through the lands of Egypt and Northern Africa to the mountains where dwelt the fishermen of the jars. "Wise words, O Talib," said the Caliph, "let thee be our messenger and I will give thee letters of passage to our brothers in Egypt and Morocco that they might use thee well, and I will care for thy house and thy family and thy belongings whilst thou art gone."

"With love and gladness, O Commander of the Faithful," said Talib, for he lusted after the possibility of treasure, and he forthwith gathered to him the men and money which the Caliph had assigned, and he rode out to meet whatever fate the Hand of Allah might hold for him.

Of the Black Castle

Talib with his caravan of footmen and horsemen crossed the desert country between Syria and Egypt, where he was received with high honour by the Emir Musa bin Nusayr, the Caliph's viceroy in all the lands of North-West Africa. And when the Emir had read the Caliph's letter he determined that he too would accompany Talib on his journey, taking with him the Sheikh Abd al-Samad, an ancient man, well-shotten in years and broken down with lapse of days, but yet one who was much travelled in the wastes and wolds where they must go.

"I hear and obey the bidding of the Commander of the Faithful," said Abd al-Samad, when they consulted him on preparations for the journey, "but know, O Emir, that the road we take is long and difficult, a journey of two years going and two years returning, with the ways few and full of terror and of things wonderful and marvellous. It behoves thee, therefore, to appoint a man of wisdom to rule in thy stead, for who knows if we shall ever return."

So the Emir Musa made his son Harun governor during his time of absence,
and under the guidance of Abd al-Samad they rode westward with a great train
of camels and a thousand water-jars. (For the Sheikh had warned them that in
the crossing of the desert of Cyrene they would travel in a silent land, bereft of
all water and plagued by the hot winds of the Simoon that would parch their
water-skins before ever they were half way across.) And so they travelled,
through lands of plenitude and waste lands, for a year's space, until one
morning, after they had ridden all night, the Sheikh found himself in a
country which he knew not. "Truly, there is no Majesty and no Might save in
Allah," he said, "but we have wandered from our road."

"How can that be?" asked the Emir.

"The stars were overclouded and I could not guide myself by them."

"Then where on God's earth are we now?"

"I know not," said Abd al-Samad, "for I never set eyes on this land until
this moment, but we can do nothing but fare forward and trust to Allah to
guide us."

Thus it was that they journeyed on until they reached a wide land, as it were
a calm sea of grass, and away on the horizon there rose some great thing, high
and black, in the midst of which a smoke seemed to rise and hang over the
confines of the sky. So they rode across the plain, day and night, in the
direction of this dark shapelessness, and as they approached it, lo! it became a

high castle, built like a mountain, all of black stone, with lowering battlements and a gate of gleaming China steel that dazzled the eyes and wits of those who looked upon it. Round about it were a thousand steps, while what had seemed to be smoke was a vast central dome, built of lead, an hundred cubits high.

"Indeed, there is no God but Allah!" cried the Sheikh Abd al-Samad, "for I know this to be the Black Castle, and I tell you that from here our way lies across country to the City of Brass, whence it will be an easy journey along the sea-coast, past the wells and watering-places of the ancient Emperor Iskander to the country that you seek. But first let us go and look in yonder palace, for its marvels are an admonition to those who would be admonished."

So the Emir went up to the castle with Talib and the Sheikh and with his officers and men and behold, the gate was open and over its lintel there shone in letters of gold these words:

'Welcome, O traveller, to these halls of stone;
Enter and find that which is only True:
No matter what your gear, your retinue,
You must depart just as you came—alone.'

[96]

"May Allah comfort us!" said the Emir, and he led his men one by one through the marble portico into the castle. What they found there was a scene of wealth and desolation. Walking from hall to hall, from chamber to chamber, up stairways carved from granite and along passages lined with tapestries, they saw gathered together the riches of a kingdom; but there was no living soul within to take delight in these things, and over every doorway there were words of valediction. At last, under the castle-dome itself, they came upon a pavilion wherein was a long tomb, and on the tomb a tablet of China steel with the inscription that here lay the Prince Kush, the son of Shaddad, son of Ad the Great:

> 'I builded this castle and abode here a thousand years, and had
> to wife the daughters of a thousand kings and was blessed
> with a thousand sons as fierce as lions. Here I amassed
> treasures from all quarters of the earth: cisterns of red
> gold and white silver; but there fell upon us the Destroyer
> of delights and the Sunderer of societies, and day by day
> there died two of us till all the company had perished and
> the parcels of our wealth availed us nothing, nor, with all
> our gold, could we ransom for ourselves a single day of life.
> O thou who comest to this place, take warning of that which
> thou seest of the accidents of Time and the vicissitudes of
> Fortune. All, all is vision and dream.'

When he read these words, the Emir Musa wept for the passing of so brave a household, and he would not leave the palace until he had transcribed each and every *memento mori*, that our own generations might learn wisdom.

Of the Ifrit Dahish

When the Emir Musa had done with his writing and praying, the Sheikh Abd al-Samad led the caravan away from the Black Castle and into the high hills. After three days' journey they espied at the head of a valley what seemed to be a horseman, dressed in glittering armour, staring down upon them. But as they rode towards him he neither moved nor spoke, and when they had climbed up the knoll on which he stood they found him to be a statue made all of brass. On one arm he held a shield, and on the other a couched lance with a broad glittering head, and here they saw graven the words:

'O thou that comest unto me, dost thou seek the City of Brass? If so, touch thou my spear-hand and I will revolve and where my spear points when I come to rest, follow that way. No harm shall befall you if you take that road.'

So the Emir Musa touched the spear-hand of the statue, who spun like dazzled lightning and directed them to a track leading on among the hills.

After days and nights of journeying in the way that the statue had directed they came to a wide tract of open country, in the midst of which they found a gaunt pillar of black stone like a furnace chimney, and sunk to his armpits in the pillar there was a creature the like of which none had seen before. He had two great wings and four limbs, two like human arms and two like lion's paws, with claws of iron. The whole of his body was burned black from the desert sun, his hair hung about him like horses' tails and his eyes blazed like coals, slit upwards in his face, while a third eye in the middle of his forehead gave out sparks of fire.

At the sight of this chimaera the horses became restive and the men of the company turned to flee; but the Emir Musa instructed Abd al-Samad to approach the creature and question him on his condition, "For surely he is hindered from thee, and from us all, by the rock wherein he is placed." So the Sheikh drew near and called upon the monster to make explanation of himself.

"Know then," cried the Wild Thing, "that I am an Ifrit of the Jinn, by name Dahish (which is to say the Amazed One). I am placed here by the judgement of Allah, at the behest of his apostle, Solomon the King, whose rule I flouted. For it occasioned, long years ago, that I was servant to one of the sons of Iblis in his island fastness, remote from all the business of the world. And this King had an idol of red carnelian, of whom I was the guardian, so that when men came to the idol to seek instruction or consolation I would climb into its belly and bid or forbid them.

"Now the King's daughter in this island was a woman accomplished in all beauty, whose fame was such that it eventually came to the knowledge of the Lord Solomon, who at once sent messengers to our land. 'Give me thy daughter to wife,' he claimed of our King, 'and break thine idol of carnelian, in order that thou mayst turn to the One True God and that thou and I may live in amity as father and son. Otherwise I will come upon thee with an irresistible host and make thee as Yesterday, which is gone forever.' But when

he heard this message our King knew not what to do, so on the advice of his ministers he made sacrifices to the idol and called upon it for guidance.

"Well, it seemed to me that the threats of Solomon were vain threats; for we dwelt so far from his kingdom, amid such turbulent seas, and we had at our command such armies of Jinn and Ifrits that surely no harm could come to us. So I climbed into the belly of the idol and spoke words of defiance, such that our King flogged the messengers of Solomon for their insolence and bade them return and tell him to rejoice that we did not come to him with our cohorts to render him into nothing but an old tale.

"Alas! in my ignorance I knew nothing of the might of the servants of Allah, for no sooner had his messengers returned to the great King than he assembled all the forces that were under his hand: Jinn and Marids and Satans from the islands of the sea and the tops of the mountains to the number of a thousand thousand, a great army of kings with their men and horses and a leashed cavalcade of lions and serpents, and over all the birds of the air to fall upon the enemy from the skies. Then Solomon seated himself upon his throne of alabaster, plated with red gold, and, calling upon the name of Allah, he commanded the wind to bear him and his forces to our island where he spoke in thunder from the clouds: 'Behold, I am come. Defend thyself, or break thine idol and bow down to the one God which is Allah!'

"Ah, how vain is the pride of man! For we would not heed the threats of Solomon, and we marched against him, man against man, beast against beast, and spirit against spirit. For two days the battle raged amongst the hills of our island and in the skies above, and, at the end of all, the strength of Allah prevailed and we were humbled to the dust. I myself was locked in battle with Al-Dimiryat, Lord of the Jann, a creature formed like a mountain of fire and smoke, but when I saw that our army was broken and that there was no hope more for the keeper of the idol I turned and fled through the skies.

"But Al-Dimiryat pursued me a three months' journey, and when I fell down from weariness he gathered me up and bore me to Solomon who commanded this pillar to be fashioned; and here he set me and chained me, sealing me with his signet ring, and Al-Dimiryat brought me to this desert place where I must remain till Judgement Day."

When the Emir Musa heard this tale of the Ifrit Dahish he marvelled at the power of the Emperor Solomon and he besought the monster to tell him more of the Emperor's rule, and particularly if there might be Jinn and Ifrits like himself, imprisoned and sealed in brass jars. "Yes," said the Ifrit, "indeed so, and if you follow your route across this desert to beyond the City of Brass, then shall you come to the shores of a great sea where you shall find a tribe of fishermen. Ask there for the jars that you seek."

Of the City of Brass

So the Emir Musa, with Abd al-Samad his guide and Talib bin Sahl his
companion, bade farewell to the Ifrit in his pillar of stone and fared onward
through the level sands of the desert. Nor had they gone far before they
perceived, far off, a great blackness within which there seemed to burn twin
fires. "What then is that strange sight?" asked Musa, but Abd al-Samad
answered with laughter, "Rejoice, O Emir, for that is none other than the City
of Brass, surrounded with high walls of black stone and guarded with two
towers of Andalusian brass from which it takes its name. Let us ride on."

Then they fared forward without ceasing until they drew near to the city
which seemed as though it must have been hewn out of a mountain of basalt
or moulded in black iron. Its walls and bulwarks towered unclimbable, and
though the Emir rode the city round—a journey of two days—there seemed
no sign of a gate, not even in the blinding walls of its glittering towers. "What
then must we do to gain entry to this city and its wonders?" asked Musa.

"Ah, Lord," said Abd al-Samad, "there are indeed five-and-twenty
gateways in these walls, but all are hidden and none may be opened but from
within."

At this news a wildness fell upon Talib bin Sahl, for he yearned to see what
treasures the city might contain. "Allah prolong thy fortune!" he said to the
Emir, "but why should we not make a ladder to mount the wall and then we
may perchance come at a gate from the inside through which all may enter?"

"Wisdom and understanding," said Musa, and he called for carpenters and
blacksmiths and bade them make a ladder out of wood, plated and bound with
iron, such that a man might climb to gain the high parapet of the walls. So
they chose what seemed the most accessible place and by means of complex
measurements and triangulations, they calculated that the ladder must needs
be so many hundred cubits tall with so many thousand rungs. After a month's
labour the joiners and the blacksmiths completed their toil and when all the
company laid hold of the great ladder and set it against the wall, behold! it
reached to the parapet as truly as if it had been built for it by the founders of
the city.

"Who then will mount the ladder," asked the Emir Musa, "and walk along
the wall to seek for us a gate that may be opened?" Whereupon one of the
tribesmen replied, "I will go up, O Emir, and descend and open to you," and
he forthwith mounted, rung upon rung, to the top of the ladder while all men
watched him. But when he reached the parapet he stood with arms
outstretched, gazing fixedly into the city. Then he clapped his hands and cried
in a loud voice, "By Allah, thou art beautiful!" and without more ado cast

himself down into the place.

"By Allah, thou art a dead man!" said the Emir Musa, but at once a companion tribesman came up to him saying, "O Emir, that was a mad fellow, and surely his madness got the better of him with all that climbing of the ladder. Let me go up and open the gate, for I am a man of sense and reason."

"Very well," said Musa, "go up, and may Allah go with thee." So the man mounted after his comrade to the top of the wall. When he got there he, too, stood for a moment surveying all he saw before him with outstretched arms. Then he clapped his hands together, crying, "Splendour of all splendours!" and hurled himself down into the city.

"If such be the act of a man of reason," said the Emir Musa, "then what truly will a madman do? If all our men are as reasonable as this we shall lose everyone, and none shall return from this errand to the Commander of the Faithful. Let us move on." But a third man pleaded to be given his chance to climb the ladder—and a fourth, and a fifth to the number of twelve—all claiming to be men of sense and reason, but all casting themselves to their death as did the first man of all.

Then the Sheikh Abd al-Samad came forward, bent low under his burden of years. "O Emir," he said, "this affair is reserved to none other but myself, for the experienced is not like the inexperienced. I shall climb the ladder."

"Indeed thou shalt not," said the Emir Musa, "for if thou too—experienced or no—perish as these others have perished, we shall be cut off to the last man, for thou art our guide." But the Sheikh would have none of it and crying the name of Allah, the Compassionating, the Compassionate, he mounted the ladder to its topmost rung.

When he reached the parapet he, too, spread wide his arms, so that those watching below clutched themselves and prayed for their own sakes and his, but the Sheikh laughed beyond measure and stayed for an hour upon the wall, reciting the name of Allah the Almighty and repeating the Verses of Safety. Then he rose and cried at the top of his voice to those below, "O Emir, have no fear, for Allah has averted from me all temptation. Know you that I saw here, swimming as it were in a lake below me, ten maidens with hair outflung and with bodies as the full moon, singing and calling me to join them:

> 'Weialala leia
> Wallala leialala.'

So I thought to throw myself down to be with them, but then, by my wisdom, I recalled and saw my twelve companions lying dead at the bottom of the wall, and I restrained myself and called upon Allah to protect me; for surely this was some enchantment devised by the people of the city to defend it against those who might seek to enter."

With these words the Sheikh Abd al-Samad set off along the parapet-walk until he came to the towers of brass, where he saw two gates of gold set close in the tower and without any means for their opening so that he could get down into the tower. Gazing about him, though, he perceived in the middle of one of the gates a further horseman of brass with his hand outstretched as though pointing, and in the palm of his hand were the words:

> 'O thou who comest to this place, if thou wouldst enter the tower
> turn the pin in my navel twelve times and the gate will open.'

So Abd al-Samad examined the horseman, and there in his navel was a pin of gold which he turned twelve times, whereupon the horseman reared and spun round like lightning and the gate swung open with a noise like thunder.

Abd al-Samad entered the tower and found himself in a long passage which brought him to the steps that led down to the guard-room. There, seated on benches and fully armed, with swords drawn and bows ready-notched, were the men of the guard, all dead. And beyond the guard-room were the sentries at the gate—dead too—while the gate itself was secured with iron bars and curiously wrought bolts and chains and padlocks. Within the guard-room, however, the Sheikh had spied an old man, seated upon a high wooden bench, whom he took to be the Warder of the Guard, and sure enough when he examined the old man's robe he found therein a great bundle of keys hanging at his girdle. These he took to the gate and one by one undid the locks and bolts until, with a crash like reverberant thunder, the great leaves of the gates flew open and the city was revealed to those who stood outside. "Allaho Akbar; God is Most Great!"

Then the Emir Musa greeted the Sheikh as though they had been parted many years, and making fair disposition for men to guard the gate and for others to bury the fallen bodies of their comrades, he proceeded with Abd al-Samad and Talib bin Sahl to an exploration of the city.

It was a place of mystery and wonder. For as they moved through the streets they found houses and mansions, bazaars and markets, all built from black stone and brass and all peopled with men and women who seemed to be about their daily business, except that they were dead. In the houses, servants waited by the gilded vestibules; in the markets there were traders all in their accustomed places: the silk merchants amongst their silks and brocades, the perfumers surrounded by bladders of musk and ambergris, the money-changers with their shops full of gold and silver coin—but all with their skin dried on their bones, statuesque in the sleep of death.

Then the Emir Musa and his party moved on to the palaces of the great, and they found there pavilions full of rich stuffs, jewels and precious stones, and weapons of tempered steel, while in the courtyards fountains still played and streams flowed in marble channels across the floor.

 "Indeed," said Sheherezade to the Shah Shahryar, "I am told that the floors themselves were cunningly made of veined marble, inlaid with precious stones so that they resembled a carpet of flowing water. In this they resembled a floor which the Emperor Solomon had constructed when he was wooing the beautiful Balkis, the Queen who held converse with butterflies. My Lord may remember that it was rumoured that Balkis, whatever her beauty, had legs that were hairy as those on an ass. So the Emperor Solomon called her to meet him in a chamber where he had laid down a pavement of glass over a

 stream of water with fish swimming in it. Balkis, believing it to be nothing but water, raised her skirts in order to cross and behold! the Emperor could see that the rumours were indeed true. But Balkis was wise as well as beautiful, so he loved her, hairy legs and all.''

In the innermost chamber of the palace, Musa and his comrades found a domed pavilion of stone, gilded with red gold and crowned with a cupola of alabaster, wherein was a ceremonial dais under a canopy of silk. On this dais there lay a lady who seemed to watch them coming. She was more beautiful than a clear pool in a desert oasis, clad in a body-robe of fine gauze

embroidered with pearls and wearing on her breast an amulet filled with musk and ambergris, and about her head a fillet of jewels that were worth more than the empire of the Caesars. "Peace be with thee, O lady," said the Emir Musa; but Talib bin Sahl said to him, "Allah preserve thee, O Emir, but verily this lady is dead, so how shall she return thy greeting? See, she is a corpse, wondrously embalmed, even to the glint and movement in her eyes, and so her servants too." For about the dais there were body-servants of the lady, and on the steps leading up to her couch two statuesque figures of Andalusian copper, the one holding a mace of steel and the other a sword of watered steel which dazzled the eye.

Between these sentries, on the steps to the couch, there lay a golden tablet inscribed with the following words:

'In the name of Allah, Lord of Lords and Causer of Causes!
Behold here Tadmurah, daughter of the Kings of the Amalekites
and queen of this City of Brass. Know ye that I reigned here
in wealth and wisdom as one for whom there would be no end to
the world's glory. But truly it is said:

"The Worldly Hope men set their Hearts upon
    Turns Ashes—or it prospers; and anon,
Like Snow upon the Desert's dusty Face
    Lighting a little Hour or two—is gone."

For a great famine fell upon us, with seven years of drought,
when no rain fell and no green thing came forth to sustain us,
and though we sent to every quarter of the world with our
treasure, seeking to barter pearls for grain and gold for
meal, ounce against ounce, yet gleaned we nothing. So we
despaired of help and closed the gates of our City upon the
world and committed ourselves forever to the destiny of Allah.
Take warning therefore, ye who follow here, though ye may
gather unto yourselves the riches of my people, they will
avail you nothing; nor may you lay any hand upon me and
mine, for I bide here in the mercy of Allah, an admonishment
to those who would be admonished of the transience of
earthly affairs.'

When the Emir Musa had read this doleful history he commanded that those who heeded the lure of gain more than the prophecy of loss might gather to them whatever treasures the City should afford, but that the time had now come when they should make ready to seek the final end of their journey.

"But Lord," said Talib bin Sahl, "shall we in truth leave this lady thus? For see, she has about her neck and on her brow a ransom for all the princes of the earth."

"Didst thou not read?" said Musa, "didst thou not apprehend that she makes us free of her City in order that she herself may be unmolested?"

"But Lord," said Talib again, "of what consequence are these things to her now? Behold, she is dead and a single garment of cotton is all her need."

With these words, Talib bin Sahl strode to the dais and set foot upon the steps to the couch to claim her jewels. But as he mounted, he passed between the two slaves and lo! the mace-bearer swept round and smote him on the back with his mace of steel, and the sword-bearer swung his weapon with a single movement and struck off his head, so that he fell dead upon the steps.

Of the Ending of the Journey

The Emir stayed not to mourn the killing of Talib, saying, "Allah have no mercy on thy resting place, for this is the only end to greed," and calling for the horses and the baggage train, he left the City. And as the last man crossed the threshold of the tower, the great gate crashed to behind him and the place returned to immemorial silence.

Abd al-Samad now led the caravan across the desert past the Wells of Iskander until they came to the fringe of a great sea and here they followed the coast a journey of many days. At last they came within sight of the mountainous shores of the land that they were seeking and in the caves of the mountains there dwelt the tribe of black men who spoke an unknown tongue. Among these they pitched their tents.

They had not long been encamped on the shores of the sea when a huge man, black-skinned from head to toe, came down from the caves and addressed them in their own speech, asking whence they came and whether they were men or Jinn.

"Well, we are men," said Musa, "but you, from your size and majesty, are surely a Jinni."

"That is not so," said the black man, and he went on to relate how he was king of his tribe and how he had long before encountered a prophet on the sea-shore from whom he had learned the worship of Allah, the Most High, and the speech of Mohammed, His Apostle.

"Tell me then," said Musa, "if thou knowest anything of those jars, in which the Emperor Solomon is said to have sealed half the Devils of Hell and cast them into the sea in such a place as this."

"With love and gladness," replied the chieftain, and he told how the sea-bed below his cliffs was littered with such jars; then, in course of preparing a royal welcome for his guests, he sent divers down to the sea bottom and before his hospitality was at an end they had brought up fifty jars, sealed at the mouth, and impressed with the ring of Solomon.

So after much feasting, and the exchange of many gifts, Musa bin Nusayr and the faithful Sheikh Abd al-Samad turned their caravan towards Damascus. After long months of travel without mishap, they entered at last the great gate of the Caliph's palace and laid before Abd al-Malik bin Marwan the treasures of their journey and the tale of their adventures, even down to the slaughter of Talib bin Sahl.

"Would that I had come with you!" cried the Caliph; and he rewarded them with riches and high honours for their devotion. And if any man came to his court after that time who spoke slightingly of the Might of Allah and the glory of his prophets, then he would call for one of the jars of Solomon, break the seal, and marvel as the imprisoned spirit spired into the clouds crying repentance to the heavens.

And when she had concluded the Story of the City of Brass, Sheherezade told the Shah Shahryar many tales and anecdotes that she had heard from the men of the desert and from the dwellers in towns. And among these tales there was the tale of:—

THE MAN WHO STOLE THE DOG'S GOLDEN DISH

There was once a merchant who had fallen upon hard times. His debts grew and his debtors sought to have him imprisoned—so he left his home and his family and wandered at random across the wide world. One day he came to a fine city and met in the main street a company of young men, roistering up and down; so he joined them and followed them to a house of such magnificence that it might have been a royal palace, with domes and turrets reaching to the sky. In went the roisterers and in went our merchant and they walked through corridors and vestibules and saloons until they came to a great chamber, where sat the Lord of the House, a majestic and dignified man, surrounded by pages and eunuchs and slaves.

Perplexed by the scene, and ashamed of his ragged appearance, the merchant withdrew to a far corner of the room where he watched the feasting and festivities of the crowd. And while he was standing there, behold, a servant came in with four great hounds—each with a silver leash and a collar of gold about its neck. The dogs were fastened to one of the carved pillars of the hall, and the servant went out and returned with four golden dishes, piled with rich meat—one for each of the dogs.

The merchant watched in amazement as the creatures set about taking their dinner, and so hungry was he that he longed to join them and share their meat. And so it occurred that one of the dogs turned to look at him and was inspired by Allah the Almighty to recognize the sadness of his case; and the dog drew back from the dish and signed with his paw to the man to come and eat his meat; and when he had finished the dog pushed the golden dish towards him with his fore-paw, as though telling the man that he should take it, so he did so and left the house and went his way with no one following him.

The merchant journeyed on to another city, where he sold the dish—laying out the money he received on goods which he sold and traded with until once more he became a man of wealth. He returned to his own town, paid off his

debts, and rose to become one of the most prosperous men in those parts.

After some years had gone by he decided that he should return to the city where he had found such good fortune and repay the Lord for the dish that he had stolen. So he furnished himself with money and with suitable presents and journeyed by day and night until he reached the place that he sought for. There was the town, there was the main street where he had met the roistering company—but when he came to the mansion-house he found only ruins. The domes and turrets had fallen in and crows walked amongst the rubble.

"Truly," said the merchant to himself, "there is no constancy and no might save in Allah:

> 'The fretted filigree is turned to rust,
> Masters and servants now alike are dust!'"

and while he was musing thus he saw a wretched man, dressed only in a ragged gown, poking in the ruins with a stick.

"Ho, thou!" said the merchant, "what has become of this place and of the great Lord who held court here but a few years ago?"

"Here he is," said the beggar-man; "I am he, and this was my mansion—which lies now as a lesson to those who will learn and a warning to those who will be warned that Allah raises up nothing of this world except He cast it down again."

And the man went on to tell of the days of his wealth and how all the world paid him court—until one day he missed a golden platter that was used to feed his hunting-dogs. Such was his rage and frenzy at this loss that his friends gradually moved against him. Fortune turned away from all his dealings, and his future now lay in the broken remnants of his palace.

"In Faith," said the merchant, "do not despair, for I have brought you the recompense of that golden plate and a bountiful token of my gratitude beside." And he told the ragged Lord the story of how the dog offered him the dish and how he used it to regain his affluence and that he was now come to repay his debt of honour.

"Go thy ways," said the Lord; "it was the dog gave thee the dish, and how should I stand debtor to one of my own dogs? I will take nothing from you—not even the parings of your finger nails." And with that he returned to poking in the ruins with his stick.

"But this tale," said Sheherezade, "is not so cheering to the spirit as another that I know, which is:—

THE TALE OF THE RUINED MAN AND HIS DREAM

There lived once in Baghdad in a house beside a grove of pomegranate trees a great merchant. But, as with the one who got the golden dish, hard times came upon him too and it was all that he could do to earn a poor living by carrying other people's goods about the streets.

Now one night, while he slept, a Speaker came to him in a dream and said, "Behold! your fortune is in Cairo; go there and find it." So he set out for Cairo, and after many days travelling he reached the city, and because it was evening he went in to a mosque to sleep.

He had not been there long before a band of thieves passed through the shrine intent upon robbing the house next door. But the owners heard them at their work and cried aloud for the protection of the law so that the thieves ran off—and when the men-at-arms arrived whom should they find but our merchant sleeping in the mosque. They took him up, beat him with palm rods till he was nearly dead and then threw him in prison, where he lay three days and three nights.

Then came the magistrate: "Who are you and what brought you to Cairo?" he said.

And the merchant answered, "I am an honest merchant from Baghdad, fallen upon evil days. A Speaker came to me in a dream and told me that my fortune was in Cairo and that I should go there to find it—but all the fortune I have found is the bunch of palm rods that you so generously gave me!"

So the magistrate laughed and said, "What a foolish fellow you are to put your trust in shadows. Why, three times now I have myself heard a voice saying to me in a dream, 'Go you to Baghdad and there, under the fountain in the courtyard of such and such a house beside a grove of pomegranate trees you shall find great treasure', but do you think that I am so stupid as to go traipsing so far merely at the behest of a dream?"

So he gave the man money to return home, and the man did so with all speed, for he knew the grove and the house and the courtyard and the fountain for his own. And when he got back he dug beneath the fountain and found there a great store of gold and pearls and rubies, just as the magistrate had foretold; so he lived in peace and contentment all the rest of his days.

 "But this tale," said Sheherezade, "is still not so cheering to the spirit as others which I know," and she proceeded to recount many anecdotes about the fond and the foolish. Among these she told:–

THE TALE OF THE SIMPLETON AND HIS DONKEY

A simple fellow was walking along the road one day, leading his donkey, when it was his misfortune to pass by two rogues. ''I will have that fellow's donkey,'' said the first rogue.

''Fame and fortune to you if you do,'' said the second, and he watched while his companion crept along level with the donkey and then, when the simpleton wasn't looking, hooked off the donkey's halter and put it over his own head; and he walked along as though he were the donkey, while his companion made off with the animal itself.

When he saw that they'd got clean away the first rogue stopped stock still. The simpleton pulled the halter, pulled again, and then turned round to see what was the matter. He was amazed to discover that he'd got a man on the end of his rope. ''What art thou? Tell me,'' he said; and the rogue replied,

''Why, I am thy donkey, but first I was a man (as now). Hear my story, and let it be a warning to you to repent of all transgression. For you must know that, in time past, I was a terrible drunkard, and when the wine was hot upon me I used to beat my poor old mother. Well, one day she called upon the Almighty to avenge her, and Allah turned me into a donkey—but now that my mother's end approaches she must have pleaded to have me restored to my former shape."

"Truly," cried the simpleton, "there is no majesty and no might save in Allah, the Glorious and Great. May Allah be with thee now, O my brother, and may he acquit me of all injury I may have done thee, riding thee about the land, and beating thee, and so forth." And he let the rogue go (who returned to his comrade) and went home to his wife; and they made offerings and gave alms to atone for their having treated a man as though he were a donkey.

When this time of contrition was over, the simpleton's wife sent him off to the market to get them another donkey so that they might continue their trade. When he got there, though, he was astonished to find his own old donkey among the creatures that were being put up for sale. Privily, when no one was looking, he sidled up to the beast and whispered in its ear, "Woe to thee, thou ne'er do well. Drunk again—and beating thy mother! But by Allah I will not rescue thee this time." And he bought a beast that seemed to him of a more sober constitution.

And, amongst all these anecdotes, Sheherezade also told:—

THE TALE OF JA'AFAR THE BARMECIDE AND THE AILING BEDOUIN

It came about that one day Harun al-Rashid, the Commander of the Faithful, was walking in the desert with Abu Ya'kub, his Cup-bearer, and Ja'afar, his Wazir, and they encountered an old Bedouin propped up upon his ass.

"Question him," said the Caliph to Ja'afar, "and see if you can bring us some entertainment in this dry desert."

So Ja'afar went up to the Bedouin and asked him where he came from and whither he was going. "I am from Basra," said the old man, "and I am going to Baghdad, there to find a medicine for my eye."

"Well met, then, well met!" cried the Wazir, "for behold! you have encountered the vendors of the finest eyewash in the land. What will you requite us if we prescribe a remedy for your ills?"

"Why," said the Bedouin, "I will seek to pay you exactly what your remedy is worth."

"Here is your prescription then," said Ja'afar. "You must take three ounces of wind, three ounces of sunbeams, three ounces of moonbeams and a small pinch of lamplight. Mix these well together and let them lie in a dark place for three months. Then place them in a mortar without a bottom for another three months, after which you must pound them to a fine powder. After trituration has set in, leave them in the air in a mixing bowl for a further three months, when they shall be ready. Apply the medicine three drams a night while you are asleep and, Inshallah, you shall be healed and whole in a trice."

Now after the Bedouin had heard this prescription to the end, he stretched himself out on his donkey's back and let fly a terrible fart which resounded across the desert wastes. "Behold!" he cried, "due payment for thy medicine." And the Caliph Harun al-Rashid was so pleased with his answer that he ordered him three thousand silver pieces.

Now on the last night of telling these anecdotes, when
Sheherezade was done, she perceived that the dawn was still
below the horizon and she told the Shah Shahryar of an
unusual event. Some time before, it seems, passing incognito
through the market-place on her way to the hammam baths,
she had encountered a crowd of people listening to stories from
a traveller, recently arrived. He was a stranger from the north,
speaking a rustic dialect, but he told stories that he said were
famed in his territory; and Sheherezade had attended to the
tales that he told. "Now my Lord," she said to the Shah
Shahryar, "from my recollections of this man, let me seek to
copy something of his strange speech and recount to you the
stories that he told." And as the nights passed, Sheherezade
told the Shah:—

THE STORY OF ALI BABA AND THE FORTY THIEVES

The Cave

One time, many years back, there were two brothers: one a jolly man, round as a sweet apple, who was called Ali Baba; the other thin, and mean as a creaking door, and he was called Kasim. Kasim had married a woman as stingy as himself—the daughter of a merchant down in the market—and when that one took his trade to Heaven, Mr and Mrs Kasim continued in his place and they just got meaner and meaner, and richer and richer.

As for Ali Baba though, he had married a feckless, prodigal lady and they never had a penny to their names. Every day Ali Baba would take three asses into the nearby forest, where he would load them up with brushwood and dry timber to sell round the streets, but whatever he earned he and Mrs Ali Baba would spend, living the good life.

Well, one day he was sitting in the forest, munching a pitta bread sandwich for his dinner, when he heard a jingling of bridles and felt the ground beneath him quiver with the tread of horses' hoofs: many horses, many hoofs. So being a prudent chap—especially when pitta bread sandwiches were on the go—and thinking that this might be a notorious band of forest outlaws, he pushed his asses deep into the undergrowth and shinned up a nearby tree, to be well out of sight when they came along.

And just as well that he did. For this was indeed a bunch of robbers—forty men with horses and baggage and who knows what—and as they got to the tree where Ali Baba was hiding they stopped and their Chief went up to a wall of rock that rose out of the forest floor opposite the tree. The Chief looked at the wall of rock. The wall of rock looked at the Chief. Then the Chief said, "Open, Sesame!"—and straightway, with a noise like a thousand grind-stones, part of the rock slid aside to make a great doorway, and the Chief and his men rode inside with their baggage. Then the rock slid closed behind them.

"Allah protect us all," said Ali Baba up in his tree; and he stayed there, not daring to finish his dinner and hoping that his asses wouldn't start braying, for fear he'd be discovered and done away with on the spot. Eventually the rock-door slid open again and the Chief, their captain, rode out, stopping on the threshold to count the men who followed him—one to thirty-nine. When he was sure they were all there he turned to the rock and said, "Shut, Sesame!" and the door slid to and the robbers trotted away.

When he was sure they were all gone, Ali Baba came down from the tree, reckoning to get home as fast as he could. But when he saw the rock-wall, standing there so inviting-like, he couldn't stop himself from saying, "Open, Sesame!" and—squeak, grind, rumble—the door opened for him too.

Well, that could clearly be taken as a sign—from Earth, if not from Heaven—so Ali Baba stepped into the cleft to see what he could see. Sheesh! High up in the ceiling of the rock there had been fashioned cunning air-holes and bullseye windows, and by the light that streamed down Ali Baba could see great bales of embroidered cloths, camel-loads of silks and brocades, mounds of carpets, and bags and sacks full of gold and jewels. Surely not just this band of robbers, but their fathers and grandfathers must have been hiding their loot in this cave for more years than they had donkeys.

Although the rock-door had rumbled shut behind him when he'd got inside the cavern, Ali Baba kept calm, and after he'd looked at all the heaps of treasure he turned and said, "Open, Sesame!" and the door obediently rumbled open. Thereupon he went and found his three asses, brought them to

the cave and loaded them with sacks of gold, hidden by a covering of brushwood and kindling. Then he said, "Shut, Sesame!" and made off back home as fast as his poor tottering animals would let him.

The Kitchen Scales

When Ali Baba got to the yard by his house he drove in the asses and carefully shut the gate so no one would see what he was up to. Then he began to unload the covering of brushwood so that he could get at the gold. But Mrs Ali Baba, hearing the coins clink and feeling the heavy, knobbly leather bags, straightway thought her man had been up to no good and went to fetch her rolling-pin so that she could talk to him about living an honest life.

Before she could get into the swing of her lecture though, Ali Baba explained what had happened and poured out on the kitchen table some of the golden dinars and sovereigns and asrafis that he had collected from the cave. This caused her to have second thoughts about questions of honesty, and, being of an orderly disposition, she began to count up the coins and stack them according to their values.

"You daft duck," said Ali Baba, "you'll never get through with that all night, and we'll have money piled up to the ceiling. Why don't we just dig a nice hole in the floor and tip it all in; then we can call on it whenever we want a treat."

"Well, you're right," said his wife, "but even so it would be nice to know roughly what we've got. Why don't we weigh it? I'll go round and borrow Mrs Kasim's scales and I'll weigh the stuff while you're digging the hole."

So Mrs Ali Baba went round to her sister-in-law's and asked to borrow her kitchen scales. "Funny," thought Mrs Kasim, "funny. She's never been that wild about cooking before; what's she after with these scales?" and while she pretended to hunt them out from the bottom of a cupboard she secretly smeared some honey over the pan of the balance. "That should tell us something," she said to herself.

Well, the Ali Babas got on with their weighing and their digging, and when they'd finished they carefully stowed all their winnings away under the kitchen floor and Mrs Ali Baba took the scales back to Mrs Kasim—and of course she hadn't bothered to wash them up or anything before she left. So when Mrs Kasim came to inspect them, once Ali Baba's wife had gone home, what should she see stuck to the golden honey but a golden coin. "Asrafis!" she yelled, "asrafis! Those good-for-nothing Ali Babas—they've not just laid hold of some cash somewhere, but they're having to weigh out asrafis on my scales as though they were corn husks!" And when old squinty Kasim came back from his shop, she told him what had happened and packed him off round to his brother's to find out what was the beginning and end of it all.

"What's this, then?" said Kasim to Ali Baba. "Just look at you. Holes in your best tunic—and yet you have to borrow my wife's scales to weigh out your gold. What's going on?"

"Don't know what you're talking about," said Ali Baba.

"Look at this then," said Kasim; and he held up the asrafi, still sticky with honey. "Now, what's going on?"

Well, Ali Baba had known his brother and his brother's wife long enough to judge when he could make monkeys out of them and when he couldn't, and this time he saw was a time for plain-dealing. He told Kasim about his adventure in the forest and his discovery of the robbers' gold and how he'd brought back a bag or two to take care of. But that wasn't enough for Kasim.

"If you don't tell me exactly where that place is, and exactly what I have to do to get in, then I'll take you round to the magistrate tomorrow and you can explain to him how you came by so much gold."

Kasim's Come-uppance

There was nothing to be done about it. Ali Baba had to tell his brother the exact whereabouts of the cave in the forest, and the exact password for getting into it; and the next day Kasim hired a dozen mules and set off to see what he could see. Everything fitted: track through the forest; clearing; wall of rock; and the magic words. "Open, Sesame!" said Kasim, and the door rolled backwards and in he went with his bags and satchels to collect up whatever winnings he could find.

As was usual, the rock-door had rumbled shut behind Kasim when he'd gone in; but after he'd stuffed all his baggage full of gold and jewels and suchlike he couldn't for the life of him remember how to get it open again. "Open, Barley!" he said—recollecting that the magic had to do with some sort of seed—"Open, Millet! Open, Poppy-head!" (and even, in a reckless effort to be funny, "Open, Cumin!"). But it was all to no avail. The door stayed shut, nor did he have any hope of climbing the smooth walls of the cave up to its high windows. The gold in his sacks glinted at him like grinning teeth.

Then he heard a commotion outside. For the robber band, riding past their hide-out, were surprised to see a great team of mules browsing around outside the door—for Kasim had foolishly not bothered to tether them in the under-brush the way Ali Baba had done. The Captain rode up to the door and Kasim, wild with anguish, heard him yell the magic words, "Open, Sesame!" and the rock began to trundle sideways. What could he do? Hoping to gain something from surprise he rushed out of the cave as soon as there was a gap wide enough for him to do so, but, alas! he ran full tilt into the Captain, and before the door had finished its opening the robbers had thrown him to the ground and chopped him in half.

They were dumbfounded. How could this stranger have found his way into their lair? How had he known of their riches, that he'd brought all these sacks to carry them away? Who else might be in the know?

Well, one thing was for sure. If this burglar had got any accomplices then they'd better look out. So the Captain ordered his men to divide up the two bits of Kasim's dead body and they hung two quarters of Kasim outside the door and two quarters inside as a warning to those who would be warned.

Coping with the Corpse

Back at home, Mrs Kasim was getting more and more worried. By the time it got dark and her man not back yet, she went round to Ali Baba's to see what might be done. "Twelve mules," she said, "and all those sacks; we must be able to find him somewhere." And Ali Baba tried to comfort her and promised that he'd start off on a search as soon as it was light.

This he did. He took some of his own asses and made off like he was collecting firewood as usual, and he headed for the robbers' cave. As soon as he got there and saw the bloody bits of Kasim hanging outside the door he settled that his brother wasn't such a bright chap after all and—taking a chance that no one was inside—he called to the door to open.

Well, when he saw the other bits of Kasim, and Kasim's sacks still full of gold in there, he realized what had happened. He straightway bundled as much as he could of his brother and his brother's treasure into his own sacks, covered everything with brushwood, and set off home. He didn't fancy giving the lads a second chance with their cleavers.

When he got home he handed over the sacks of gold to his wife to take care of, and then he took the asses round to Kasim's house to break the bad news to Mrs Kasim. Knock, knock: he tapped at the door. But the door was opened not by Mrs Kasim but by Morgiana, her body slave, who was a pretty bright lass, and as soon as she'd let him in to the courtyard, Ali Baba told her the whole dreadful story.

"Brother of my lady's lord," said Morgiana, "this is thorny brushwood you are tangling with. I have some knowledge of that Captain and his men, and when they find out that someone has called in to collect Kasim and all his gold they won't rest till they have found him. We must act with the greatest circumspection."

By this time Mrs Kasim had also appeared in the courtyard, and when they broke the news to her about the dismemberment of her poor husband, they were hard put to it to stop her going at once into the street and setting up an instant wake. But Ali Baba promised that he would marry her himself, once the time of her mourning was over (for such is the custom of that place), and together they listened to the plan that Morgiana had devised.

This is how it happened. When morning came, Morgiana went down to the druggist's stall in the bazaar, seeking powerful medicine for a dangerous sickness. "Who is so ill that he needs this?" asked the druggist; and Morgiana told him it was her master. The next day she went there again and asked him for a repeat prescription, and the druggist shook his head sagely, as much as to say that no help could be expected when things were in a case like that.

That, of course, was exactly what Morgiana had intended, and it therefore came as no surprise to Kasim's neighbours and to all the merchants in the bazaar when, next day, Morgiana declared that her master was dead and that his wife and his brother and the wife of his brother were prostrate with grief.

To her had fallen the business of preparing the funeral.

Well, those preparations were not exactly conventional. That night Morgiana betook herself to the shop of one Baba Mustafa, a tailor and maker of shrouds and grave-cloths, a man well-shotten in years. Knocking at his door she proffered him a gold piece and asked him if he would accompany her on a secret journey. This he was not inclined to do and it took another asrafi before he allowed her to blindfold his eyes and lead him through streets and byways into the house and into the darkened room where the remains of Kasim were lying.

"Well, master tailor," said Morgiana, "out with your needle and sew me up this body as good as new; then when you've done, take this cloth and make me a shroud for him, for he must be buried tomorrow." So Baba Mustafa set to with his needle and by the time that all was finished he was glad enough to accept a purseful of asrafis and to allow himself once more to be blindfold and led back through the streets and alley-ways to his tailor's shop.

Calcification

Meanwhile, there was consternation among the forty thieves. For when they returned to their cave after a day of the usual villainies they found not only that Kasim-outside-the-door, but also Kasim-inside-the-door, had disappeared—and all his sacks of booty too. The secret of the Open Sesame was known, but how could they discover the knower?

"A plan, Captain," said one of the gang, and went on to explain how he might dress up like a foreign merchant and go into the town seeking information about who had died recently and who had fallen upon easy times. That way they might be able to work out who their sneaky visitor had been.

"Very well," said the Captain; so the fellow burrowed about among their bags of garments and turbans and sashes until he had got himself up to look like some wealthy trader from out of town. Then he set off for the bazaar, getting there first thing in the morning so that he could see as many of the merchants as possible.

Not much was doing when he arrived—most of the shops were still shut up—but there, sitting in the dawn light was Baba Mustafa, sewing away to catch up with the time he'd lost while he'd been attending to Kasim. "Well," said the robber, "what are you up to then? How can you see to sew stitches before it's properly light?"

"Oho," said Baba Mustafa, "it's plain you're not from these parts, I've been known for my sharp eyes longer than you've been born. Why d'y'know, someone even came along the other day to get me to sew up the bits of a dead body in a room without any light at all. And I made the chap's shroud too."

"You're joking," said the robber. "You're a tailor, not a surgeon. How could you do a thing like that?"

"Never you mind," said Baba Mustafa, "it's nowt to do with you."

"Well I do mind," said the robber, clinking a couple of gold pieces in the palm of his hand, "I'd just like to see that place where you did a thing like that."

"Well, that's not easy," said the tailor, "because I never saw it. Whoever wanted the job done put a blindfold on me and took me through the streets as if I were a nervy horse."

"Hmm," said the robber, and he put down his asrafis by the tailor's stool. "Now what about this. If I were to blindfold you too, and start you off from here, why shouldn't someone with your sharp eyes have a sharp memory too, and why shouldn't you be able to remember how the journey went?"

And that's just what occurred. The robber put one of his sashes round the tailor's eyes, and the tailor slowly retraced the steps that he'd made when Morgiana led him; round corners, down alley-ways, right to the front door of Kasim's house. "That's the one," he said, "that's where they live—and very generous they were too—good pay I got for traipsing round here and doing all that work." Which hint was taken by the robber, who gave Baba Mustafa a little bag of dinars and wished him good tailoring for the rest of his days. Then, when Mustafa had left the street, the robber pulled a piece of chalk out of his wallet, chalked a big white cross on Kasim's door and went back to report to his Chief down in the forest.

A few minutes later, out comes Morgiana to do the day's shopping. She couldn't help noticing that someone had lately put a big white cross on the front door, and, having a suspicious turn of mind, it struck her that that someone might be up to no good. So she went back indoors and found a piece of white chalk and she went round the street putting crosses on everyone's doors.

[131]

Thus it came about that when the robber came back to the town with the Captain, all ready to show him the house, he found a streetful of chalk-marks and couldn't for the life of him decide which was his and which was not. So the Captain, in a fine fury, hauled him off back to the forest and had his head chopped off for being a pestiferous nuisance, and thereupon sent Robber Number Two to see if he could do any better.

Well the same thing happened to Robber Number Two as to Robber Number One. He found Baba Mustafa, jingled gold pieces at him, got shown the house, and this time, with a touch of genius, he made a red cross immediately next to the original white one. Then he went back to the forest—and Baba Mustafa went back to his shop with a growing belief that golden asrafis were being shovelled up like desert sand.

Unfortunately for Robber Number Two the same sequence of events didn't leave off there. For once again Morgiana spotted the mark on the door and once again she found some chalk to match, so that when the man proudly brought his Chief down the street, he was dismayed to see that red crosses now adorned all the doorways, along with the white ones. The house remained inscrutable and there was nothing for it except a return to the forest and off with his head as well.

The Captain's Craft

By this time the Captain was starting to have doubts about the intelligence of his troops, so he decided that he would go and find the house for himself (at least he couldn't chop his own head off if he missed it). Thus more tours of the streets were made; more gold pieces slid into the hands of Baba Mustafa; but the Captain took no pains to mark the door but rather marked inside his head the whole placing and appearance of the house so that he would recognize it again. Then he went back to his men and propounded the following plot:

"Comrades: I have no doubt that I have found the house where is lodged the source of all our trouble and I'm going to propose an assault that will settle accounts for good. All forty of us—uh—no—sorry—um—all thirty-eight of us will travel to the town this evening. I shall travel as a sheikh dealing in oil and I shall take with me twenty—er—nineteen mules, each with two jars yoked across its back. One of these jars will indeed be filled with oil, but the other thirty-seven will contain your goodselves, comfortably stowed, and armed with scimitars, cutlasses, daggers or whatever weapons best take your fancy. We will gain admission to the house and in the dark hours of night I shall release you from your jars and we shall rise up and slay the whole household."

So it was. The oil-sheikh and his mule train rode down to the city and by tortuous journeyings made their way to Kasim's house where Ali Baba and Mrs Ali Baba were now living. (They were enjoying themselves as never before, being looked after by Morgiana and Kasim's other servants and helping Mrs Kasim to get accustomed to her grief and to the prospect of becoming another wife for Ali Baba.)

As the Captain and his entourage came up to the house Ali Baba himself was there, strolling to and fro enjoying the evening air after his supper. The Captain salaamed. "My lord," he said, "many and many a time I have come to this town selling my oil, but never before have I arrived so late. I am perplexed as to where I might rest for the night, unburden my mules and give them their fodder. Is it possible that we could tarry here in your courtyard?"

Well, Ali Baba was by nature an hospitable man and liked nothing better than company, so he welcomed the oil-sheikh to his courtyard and gave orders to Morgiana to prepare supper and a guest room for the traveller. (Nor did Ali Baba in any way recognize the sheikh for who he was. The disguise was perfect, and, in any case, he had only seen and heard the Captain before when he'd been perched up in that tree with his teeth rattling and his ears humming.)

The Captain made much ado of feeding his mules and unloading his jars. As

he did so, he whispered to each of his men that he was to wait for a summons in the middle of the night, when they should all rise from out their jars and slaughter the household. Then the Captain went indoors to enjoy his supper.

The Kitchener's Craft

Now it so happened that, half-way through the evening, while Morgiana was doing the dishes, the lamps began to flicker and fail (it's a well-known characteristic of lamps that when one goes they all go). When Morgiana went to her cruse to replenish the supply she was dismayed to discover that the cruse was empty. A black night threatened.

"What's the worry?" said Abdullah, one of the skivvy-boys, "there's thirty-eight jars of the stuff out there in the courtyard; I'm sure our friend won't miss a ladle or two off the top of one of them." So Morgiana picked up the cruse and went out to where the thirty-eight jars were lined up and began to see if she could find one that would open. Well—you can guess she was a bit startled when, first jar that she came to, she heard a voice whispering out at her, "Is it time now?" (for the chap in the jar thought she was the Captain coming to start things moving). But Morgiana came to her senses pretty quick, realized that this was not a customary thing for oil-jars to say, and replied huskily, "No; the time is not yet." And so it went on. Jar by jar she walked down the courtyard, each time hearing, "Is it time now?" and each time replying, "No; the time is not yet," till she got to the last jar of all, where she found what she'd first come to seek.

"May Allah protect us, the Compassionating, the Compassionate," she said to herself as she filled the cruse. "My lord has given lodging to this sheikh and it seems that this sheikh is going to pay him out with a mule train of bandits"; and when she got back to the kitchen she trimmed her lamps and set a great cauldron to heat on the fire. Then she took Abdullah with her out to the yard, and between them they manhandled the one full jar of oil into the kitchen and tipped it all into the cauldron.

By dint of much stirring and stoking the oil soon began to seethe and bubble in the cauldron. Morgiana then ladled some of its contents into a can, went out to the courtyard and tipped the contents into the first jar, scalding the fellow in it to death. And so, can by can and jar by jar, she went down the line of thirty-seven thieves, making an end of each and every one of them.

Not long after this, the Captain roused himself up, opened his window, and cracked his whip out over the courtyard as a signal that the assault should begin. Nothing happened. He cracked the whip again. Still nothing.

[137]

So cursing his men for falling asleep, but fearing to make too much row, he crept out to the yard to take matters into his own hands. When he got out there, though, he was startled by the smell of oil and seething flesh, and when he touched the first jar he found it reeking hot and he realized that his plot was discovered and that of all the forty thieves he was now the last one left. There was nothing for it but to make his escape as quick as he could, so he climbed over the garden wall and made the best of his way back to his cave to think up some new stratagem for revenge.

Next morning, when Ali Baba passed through the courtyard, he was surprised to see the mules still stabled and the jars still waiting to be taken to the market. He sent for Morgiana and asked her to rouse the sheikh who must surely have overslept. "No oil-sheikh he," said Morgiana, "but a bandit-chief, and it's his men who are sleeping." And she took Ali Baba down the line of jars, showing him their contents and telling him all that had happened. They settled between them that, what with the crosses on the doors and the trick with the oil, they were up against the gang of the forty thieves, but what had happened to the Captain and the other two was more than they could tell.

"We may have done for them at the moment," said Morgiana, "but I don't reckon that's the last we'll see of that Captain." With that, she and Ali Baba went down to the tool shed, picked out a couple of shovels, and dug a large pit where they quietly buried their intruders.

How It Ended

Once again Morgiana was right, of course. The Captain sat in his cave for a few days, brooding on his bad luck, then he gathered up some of his stock of silks and embroidered cloths and took himself off to the town in the guise of a merchant. He rented a pitch in the bazaar and started trading.

Well, as the days and weeks went by he put himself out to be friendly to all his fellow merchants—not least to one Khwajah Hassan, who was the son of our late friend Kasim and who was carrying on with his father's business. The Captain took much pains to cultivate this young man, giving him presents and standing him hot suppers, while for his part Khwajah Hassan was flattered to be taken up by a man who seemed to know so much of the ways of the world.

Now, one day Khwajah Hassan had the idea that he would surprise the Captain with a return treat. He fixed with Morgiana that she would be ready to prepare a fancy dinner for his new friend and then—when the day's trading was over—he suggested to the Captain that they might take a little stroll together. "Let me show you some pretty bits of the Garden District," he said, and he took the Captain down those streets and alley-ways that the Captain had traversed so recently with Baba Mustafa the tailor. "What am I to do about this?" thought he to himself—and privily fingered the dagger that he always kept tucked in his sash.

When they reached Kasim's old house, where Ali Baba was still living comfortably with Mrs Ali Baba, Mrs Kasim, and all Kasim's former servants, Khwajah Hassan stopped. "Well, now," he said, "just see where we've got to. This is my uncle's house; why don't we knock on the door and see if he's in?" The Captain, still puzzled by what was going on, didn't know what to say about that, and while he was still um-ing and er-ing Morgiana opened the door and (as she'd fixed with Khwajah Hassan) straightway asked them both in to supper.

This seemed to the Captain an opportunity for revenge that had been sent direct from Allah, but he set about a canny reply. "I am beholden to the house," he said with great formality, "and to the master of the house for the honour of such hospitality, but alas, I cannot accept; allow me to depart and tarry no longer."

As he'd expected, they wouldn't hear of it, and indeed, Ali Baba himself came to the door to help prevail upon his nephew's new-found friend to give way. "Why," said Ali Baba, "we have heard such reports of your kindness and your wisdom that we would fain entertain you this evening and hear more of your adventures walking up and down in the world."

"Alas again," said the Captain, "I long to accept your gracious invitation, but you must know that I have for many years suffered an ailment of the belly and I am now ordered by my physician never to eat food with salt in it."

"What matter? What matter?" said Ali Baba, "the meats are not yet cooked. We will prepare dinner without any salt," and he hauled the Captain into the best sitting-room and ordered Morgiana to tell the cook "no salt".

"No salt?" thought Morgiana; "no salt . . . funny . . . now what kind of ailment puts a bar on salt?" and before she left for the kitchen, she looked keenly at Khwajah Hassan's guest and she understood everything. For here surely, under his smooth disguise, was the one-time oil-sheikh, one-time leader of the forty thieves, and by not taking salt with his host he would be under no obligation of custom or of the law of the Prophet, to restrain whatever violent intentions he might harbour. "So-ho!" she thought, "this fellow is up to no good and must be attended to."

As the conversation and the salt-less dinner proceeded therefore, Morgiana took care to observe the company closely, and was not surprised to see the guest of honour fussing and fiddling from time to time with his sash, where, eventually, she perceived what could only be the handle of a hidden poniard. (And, for his part, as he fussed and fiddled, the Captain thought, "How long, how long must I still endure this boring gossip? How soon can we get rid of this tiresome servant girl and her attendants, so that I can get down to the point of the evening?")

Morgiana however, besought Ali Baba that, while they enjoyed the last of their dinner, she might dance for them, the better to show zeal for their guest's entertainment and—to the Captain's great impatience—Ali Baba agreed. So Morgiana left the supper-room and went to her closet where she found a great store of muslins, such as dancers wear. She dressed herself in a transparent veiling, bound a fine turban round her head, and placed within the sash at her waist a dagger rich in filigree and jewellery. Then she found the boy Abdullah, gave him a tambourine, and ordered him to accompany her in her dance.

Thus, with Abdullah rattling the tambourine, Morgiana entered the supper-room, bowed low to the assembled company, and began to cavort round the middle of the floor. She flung veils around, rather like the historic Salome, all the time watching the glinting eyes of the Captain of the forty thieves and she saw a flicker of understanding, and as his hand moved towards his sash, she pulled out her own dagger and lunged at him, thrusting it into his heart.

Uproar! "The girl's gone mad!" cried Ali Baba. "What a way to treat a guest!" cried Khwajah Hassan. "Rattle, rattle," went the tambourine. But Morgiana drew back and bowed to everyone. "Not mad, my lord," she said to

Ali Baba, "but prudent in my master's service;" and she showed him the dagger hidden in the Captain's sash and explained the sure purpose of his refusing to eat salt.

Then Ali Baba did indeed recognize him as the man he had first seen so long ago, down in the forest, crying "Open Sesame!"; the man who had sought his hospitality as oil-sheikh and brought into his courtyard a mule train of thieves. And he blessed Morgiana for her wit and straightway married her to his nephew Khwajah Hassan who, being a son of Kasim, was hardly a match for her beauty or her intelligence. He also gathered together his old train of asses and returned to the robbers' cave to clear it of all its treasure. Then he, and Mrs Ali Baba, and she who had once been Mrs Kasim, and all the rest of them lived (as the saying goes) happily ever after.

 And when Sheherezade had told the story of Ali Baba, which she had got from the stranger from the north, she went on to tell another which she had heard from him:—

THE STORY OF ALADDIN AND THE SLAVE OF THE LAMP

The Uncle

Times past, way off in China, in the city of all cities, there was a good-for-nothing fellow called Aladdin. His dad was a tailor, of the Tuanki family, and the idea was that Aladdin would be a tailor too, but he didn't set much store by that for a game of marbles. So instead of learning his trade he hung around street corners with a lot of tykes no better than himself. If they had any money they gambled it away; if they didn't have any they were up to no good till they got some.

Having a son who racketed around like that was bad news for the tailor. He tried all ways to get the boy to shape up, but it was no good, and in the end the chap worried himself into an early grave. There was nothing for it, then, but Aladdin's mum had to sell up the shop, and the best she could do to keep the two of them out of the workhouse was to take up spinning. Not a profitable trade. She had to spin from sun-up to midnight just to pay the rent.

Now it so happened that half-way round the world, in Africa, there lived at this time a Moorish magician. He was a chap who'd spent a lot of time perfecting the arts of geomancy (which is a bit like telling fortunes from tea-leaves, but you do it with sand). Anyway, with his sand and his sand-table he'd discovered that there was a fortune to be found over in China, but that he'd probably need the help of a down-and-out ne'er-do-well called Aladdin to do some of the dirty work.

So the Moorish magician set off for China; and when he got to the city of all cities he set about making a tour of all the back streets till he should come across the Aladdin he was looking for. Well, that wasn't so hard. By this time young Aladdin's reputation as a tear-away was pretty widely known and the magician wasn't long in discovering him with his mates—tying oil-pots to a stray dog's tail, or some such monkey business.

The Moorish magician stood there watching for a bit; then he goes up to the boy, flings his arms round him, hugs him, kisses him and I don't know what-all, and says, "Aladdin! oh, Aladdin! son of my dear old brother; say hello to your long-lost uncle!"

Well—far from saying hello, Aladdin wasn't up to saying anything at all. Nobody'd ever told him that he'd got an uncle, long-lost or otherwise, and he hadn't a clue what to do next. But the uncle had. After a lot more fussing he opened up his purse and took out a handful of golden dinars. "Oh my dear nephew,'' says he, ''take these—take these as a token of all the years that have passed us by—you and me and your dear mother and father (may Allah rest his soul). Go home to your mother and give her my greetings; tell her I'm back from all my wanderings and that tomorrow night, God willing, we'll get together to talk about old times. Here—'' (pulling more dinars out of his purse), ''make sure you lay on a nice supper; and now just tell me how I get round to your house and we'll meet again tomorrow.''

So Aladdin told him where he lived and then rushed off there to give the news to his mum. She was pretty surprised to see him, because he didn't usually come home that early, and she was still more surprised when he told her about his uncle. ''What uncle?'' she said. ''First I've heard of any uncles,'' and she reckoned it was some fancy excuse to explain how he'd come by all that gold. But Aladdin stuck to his story and made so much to-do about fixing a proper supper the next night that she didn't see she'd much alternative. So she did as he suggested, laid in more steaks and jam-puddings and jars of wine than she'd seen in the last twenty years, and sat back to see what would happen.

Sure enough, next evening, there's a ring at the bell and there stands the magician. ''Good evening, Mrs Tuanki,'' says he, ''I know this is a surprise, and I know it's short notice and all that, but now I'm back, I've just got to make amends for being such a hopeless brother-in-law to you . . .'' And so he went on; and the end of it all was that she swallowed the lot (including the nice supper), and from that day on Aladdin had an uncle and the Tuanki family had three good meals a day.

The Cave

The magician worked fast to get Aladdin into a biddable frame of mind. Along with paying the back-rent and suchlike, he said he'd make some inquiries about having the boy apprenticed to the brokers down in the market—and what with promising to set him up in business and buy him some smart clothes, he soon had him trotting around like a tame poodle. They'd go into town, look at all the monuments, eat dinner, and even wander round the public bits of the Sultan's palace, while Aladdin's uncle explained to him all the hierarchies and customs of the state.

So Aladdin wasn't surprised when one day his uncle turned up and suggested a walk in the other direction. ''If you'd like to come with me into the country,'' he said, ''I'll show you a sight beside which everything we've seen together so far will be nothing''—a remark pretty well guaranteed to encourage even a slouch like Aladdin to buckle on his shoes.

Off they went. First of all through gardens at the side of the town, each with its own pretty little pavilion or pagoda, then into open country, and then into a rocky valley that led up to the hills. "What's all this about?" said Aladdin, who'd never set foot out of the city gate before this. "Why do we want to be traipsing about in this rough country when we might be having a picnic or something back in those gardens?"

"Never you mind," said his uncle, "you keep by me and you'll see gardens beyond anything the Kings of the World can manage." And he kept walking into the rocky valley.

Eventually they got to a little flat part covered with small boulders. "Right," said the magician, "now you hunt around here and find me some sticks and stuff to make a fire"—which was a pretty tall order since most of the valley-bottom was all stones. But Aladdin was really keyed-up to know what this uncle of his was up to, so he worked away more than he'd ever done before at finding whatever bits of chippings and brushwood he could. As he brought them along, the magician made him pile them up in a little circle that he'd marked among the boulders, and while Aladdin was fossicking around, he secretly poured on some powder that he'd hidden in a flask underneath his robe.

When they'd got a fair pile of tinder together the magician walked round it with his staff, conjuring smoke and fire out of the brushwood, and as the fire took hold he began to mutter cabbalistic words over it. Then, suddenly— whump!—the whole lot exploded with a force that shook the floor of the valley. Aladdin was scared out of his wits and was all for heading back to town as fast as possible, but his uncle caught him a clip round the head that just about knocked his back teeth out and caused him to tumble to the ground.

"Hey—what's that in aid of?" he said, suddenly overcome with serious doubts about how good the intentions of his new relation really were. "All right—all right—easy does it, my dear nephew," said the magician, who didn't want Aladdin running off after all the trouble he'd had to get him there. "Cruel-to-be-kind, you know. If I'm to show you all these marvels then I can't have you clearing off home before we've even started. Now look there where the fire was." And Aladdin looked—and what he saw among the ashes was a big marble slab with a large copper ring sticking out of the middle of it. "Treasure," said the magician; "treasure, buried in your name, such that you are the only one who can redeem it. Do now as I say and you'll become richer than all the Sultans of the East," and he directed Aladdin to pull up the marble slab.

Aladdin took hold of the copper ring and heaved, but the slab wouldn't budge. He heaved again till he almost bust a gut, and the slab still wouldn't budge. "Oh, Aladdin, Aladdin, son of my brother, what did I say," said the magician, "the treasure may be yours to redeem, but you can't just heave away at that slab like a navvy. Pull the ring, and as you pull, recite your name, and your father's name and your mother's name and the stone will come up."

So Aladdin pulled again, saying these names like a prayer, and lo and behold! up came the slab as though it was on oiled bearings, and there below was a dark cave with steps going down. "Bravo!" said the magician, "well done! Now here is what you must manage next:

> you must enter that cavern and go down the twelve steps before you;
> at the bottom you will find a passage-way of four secret chambers,
> and in each chamber you will find four marble tables,
> and on each table you will find four golden jars,
> and in each jar you will find gold and gems and jewels;

but don't put your hands on any of it and don't let your body or your garments or the hem of your robe touch any of it, otherwise you will be turned into a *black stone*. Instead, go carefully through each of the chambers and when you get to the end of the fourth one you will see in front of you a plain door with a copper handle. Take hold of that handle and repeat again the

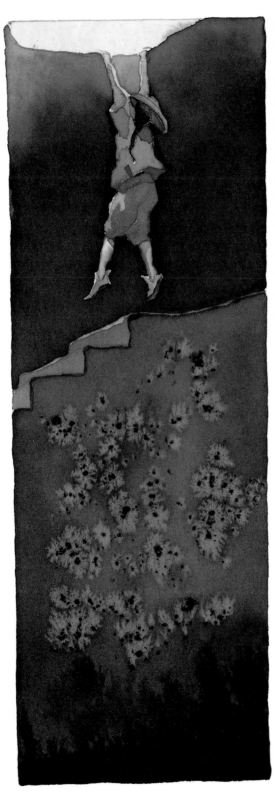

names of power and you will be able to open the door.

"The other side of the door," said the magician, "is a garden, whose like is not to be found this side of paradise. It is laid out with lawns and pathways, streams and fountains, fruit trees and flowers, of a kind beyond description—but do not be waylaid. You must take a path from the door that winds for fifty cubits until it comes to an open pavilion, and in that pavilion you will see a ladder of thirty rungs, and at the top of that ladder you will see a Lamp suspended from the roof. Climb up and take the Lamp, and once you have it tucked into your robe you shall be free of the garden and of the golden chambers. Wander where you will, take what you like, but be sure to bring the Lamp and everything back to me here at the top of the stairs.

"Go now, and for fear that any harm befalls you before you get to the Lamp take this ring, which will serve as protection so long as you keep to all that I have said," and the magician drew from off his finger his seal-ring and gave it to Aladdin.

Aladdin lowered himself down the hole until his feet reached the top step of the stairs and then he set off to follow all the directions his uncle had given him. Everything was there: the four chambers with their pots of gold, the doorway into the garden, the pathway through the trees, and the Lamp, hanging over the ladder. So Aladdin climbed up the thirty rungs, unhooked the Lamp from its gimbal, stuffed it into his robe, climbed down the thirty rungs and set off to explore the garden.

What his uncle said was true. There could surely be no other garden like this one. The grass was greener and smoother than anywhere else, the water was bluer than anywhere else, the flowers were piled up in colours more variegated than anywhere else, and as for the trees—Aladdin more or less choked. Every tree was not just more shapely than any tree he'd ever seen, but every tree also had, dangling from its branches, great clusters of glittering fruit of bewildering brilliance. Now if Aladdin had spent more time at study, or working with the merchants of the bazaar, he would have realised straightway that this fruit was not just any sort of glass bauble and crystal, but was nothing less than rare gemstones: emeralds and diamonds, rubies, spinels and balasses of a size and perfection that was ridiculous. Such things could not be possible. But Aladdin was very taken with them, so he pulled down as big an assortment of them as he could and he stuffed them into his pockets and his turban and every fold of his clothing that could carry them, and he made his way back to the staircase, rattling like a bag of marbles. He was so weighed down

with the things that there was no hope of him taking any gold from the great jars on the marble tables.

By the time he got back to the top of the stairs his uncle was pretty cross, what with hanging about up there most of the afternoon waiting for Aladdin to finish his fruit-picking. "Come on, then," he said, sharpish, when Aladdin got on to the top step, "give us the Lamp and then I'll help you climb out." Well, it was true that Aladdin needed some help: for one thing it was a big pull up out of the cave, and for another he was so weighed down with all his winnings that he was bothered how he could clamber up on his own, but he didn't see any point in passing the Lamp out first, especially since it was lodged round his belly somewhere, submerged under all the gemstones.

"Oh, no, Uncle, don't worry about that. Just give us a hand and then I'll find it for you."

"Oh, no, Nephew. Lamp first, then I'll give you a hand."

"But that's daft," said Aladdin, and went on arguing the toss until gradually he came to realize that there was more to this Lamp than he thought. His uncle obviously didn't want it just to read in bed with (and that was true, as we shall see). In the end the magician lost his head with fury and frustration. "Damn you to hell!" he cried, "*zambahshalamahzarúska!*" and with that wild and magical imprecation he caused the marble slab to fall back over the hole with a crash, nearly smashing in Aladdin's skull as it did so.

There he was, shut in the dark, while the Moorish magician tramped off down the valley and took his way back to Africa as quick as he could.

The Lamp

Aladdin was now in a right fix. He tried yelling to see if the man would let him out, but by this time he'd worked out that the wizard fellow was no uncle of his and that he was the victim of some mysterious plot, so he didn't have much hope of seeing daylight soon in that direction. But nor did he have any luck in the other direction either. With the crashing shut of the trapdoor, the doors to all the chambers and the garden crashed shut too, and Aladdin was hemmed in on his staircase in total darkness.

"Truly there is no God but The God," said Aladdin, "He sends us mirth and He sends us misery. Alhamdohlillah; praise to the All-knowing, the Omnipotent, and to his prophet Mohammed." And as he prayed these prayings he lifted his arms into the darkness, lowered them, and brought his hands together in supplication over the gemstones, rattling about in his robe.

Now as he sat there, moving his hands in prayer, it so happened that the

fingers of one hand rubbed against the ring which the magician had given him
when he first set off into the cave. And as he rubbed the ring, so there leapt
forth in a shower of bright sparks an Ifrit from the tribe of the Jann of Solomon
(for Aladdin's ring was one of those blessed with power by the great king). "Speak!"
cried the Jinni. "I am the Slave of the Ring! Speak and tell me your desires!"

Well, Aladdin was flabbergasted; one minute locked in a pitch-black dungeon
for good, the next minute asked to give orders—he didn't well know what to do.
But after goggling for a bit at the Jinni he realized that this was the best chance
he had of getting away, so he said, "Slave of the Ring, get me out of here."

Whoosh! He'd hardly blinked when he found himself sitting on the ground
above the entrance to the cavern, now all tidied over and hidden again. The
Jinni had disappeared and Aladdin decided there was nothing for it but to walk
back home and try to recover his wits a little. So he trudged off down the
valley, and past the gardens, and into the town, with all his treasures still
rattling and rolling round in his pockets and his turban and under his robe.

"Well, what happened to you?" asked his mother when he got home, "and
what's become of Uncle?"

"Don't ask me!" said Aladdin; "don't say a word!" and without more ado
he went off to his room where he unloaded all his pockets and his under-
garments into some empty jars, put the Lamp on a table, climbed into bed and
went to sleep.

Next morning, first thing, he told his mum what had occurred with his uncle. "Allah protect us!" said Mrs Tuanki, "what are we to do now? No sooner does someone come along to get you out of the gutter, teach you some manners, fix you up in a respectable job, give us some housekeeping-money, than you go and offend him so that he won't come back. That puts me back at my spinning and how we shall make out I just don't know."

"Now stop fashing," said Aladdin, "and we'll sort something out. First off, you may like to know that I brought a few things back from out of that cave, and they should see us through for a while. Look at this old Lamp, for instance," fetching the Lamp out of his room, "we could polish that up for a start and we'd get a bob or two for it down at the market."

Well, that seemed quite a good idea, so his mum fetched out the lamp-cleaning stuff and Aladdin set to work to fettle it up. But no sooner had he started to polish it than there was another great flash and out came a Jinni three times bigger and three times meaner than the last one. "Speak!" he roared, so that poor Mrs Tuanki got all her spinning in a tangle. "I am the Slave of the Lamp and of all who hold the Lamp; command me and all my fellows to whatever you desire!"

This time Aladdin was beginning to get the hang of Jann and he answered, "Breakfast. Breakfast for two—the best you can manage," and in half a shake of a donkey's tail the Jinni was back with a gigantic silver tray. All down both sides of the tray there were twelve golden bowls, steaming with good things, and in the middle there were two silver goblets and two leather bottles full of old wine. "By heck," said Aladdin, "I'm ready for this," and as the Jinni vanished he went and untangled his mother, and the two of them set about their meal.

Now Aladdin's mum was not very keen on tinkering with supernatural forces, and as soon as she'd finished her breakfast she started trying to persuade Aladdin to have no more to do with them. "Take that ring and that Lamp," she said, "and throw them in the river." But Aladdin would have none of it. For one thing he thought he might get breakfasts like that every day of the week, and for another he realized that all the shenanigans with his so-called uncle had been because of the Lamp. If the chap was willing to go through all that plotting to try to get hold of it, then it must be a pretty powerful instrument.

Anyway, to keep his mother happy he decided that he wouldn't call on the Slave more than he had to. Instead he settled to try to get by more comfortably by selling off, one by one, the bowls and the goblets that the Jinni had brought. When the money was used up from selling one he'd sell the next. At first the merchants in the bazaar thought that he was an easy

pushover—probably fencing stolen goods anyway—but he gradually came to see the value of the stuff that he was bargaining with and before long he turned into a shrewd dealer. What's more, when the goods ran out he could always call up the Slave of the Lamp and order some more.

The Princess

Everything would have gone on nicely from this time forward, except that one day Aladdin was going down to the market when he heard a great racket. The Sultan's men were coming, and with them the Town Crier who was yelling, "Beware, beware! By order of the Sultan, Lord of the Time and Master of the Age, let all men leave the streets and markets and immure them in their houses; for the daughter of the Sultan, the Princess Badr al-Budur, now comes this way in train for the hammam baths. Let no man be present, upon pain of death, to see the Princess as she passes!"

Well, that was enough for Aladdin. He'd long heard of the beauty and gracefulness of the Princess, and he'd not been shut up in caves and magicked by wizards without reckoning that he could take a look at a Princess if he wanted to. So he went along to the hammam baths and he found a little cranny, at the back of the door, where he could creep in and see the Princess as she came.

Sheesh! For once the newsmongers had got it wrong in the wrong direction. Not all the reports of the Princess's beauty had quite prepared Aladdin for the revelation of her face and form as she passed by his little hidey-hole. His knees went weak with love for her and he almost fell out of concealment—which would have been the worse for him. Anyway, from that day forth there was nothing for it but he must sort out a way to marry her.

What he did was this: first of all he persuaded his mum that she was going to have to make his proposal for him. (She thought he was downright crackers, and decided that they'd both end up getting their heads chopped off, but by this time Aladdin was a pretty determined character and she had learnt to do as he told her.) Then he went into his room and began to sort out some of the fanciest jewels from those that he'd found in the cave. "Now let's have a bowl," he said to his mum, and she hunted around the house, but the best she could come up with was her big baking-bowl out of the kitchen. "That'll do nicely," said Aladdin, and he piled in the jewels, which seemed to glitter and shine all the more brilliantly for their plain setting; and he covered the lot with a blue-check table-cloth.

"Now," says Aladdin, "what I want you to do is to take this lot down to the Sultan's palace and get in the queue for the audience-chamber. They should let you in sometime this morning and you wait in there till someone calls you up to see the Sultan. Then you give him this bowl and say something on the lines of, 'O my Lord, may the blessings of Allah be upon you, my son back home wants to marry your daughter and he's sent this stuff round as a courting-present . . .' and so on, and so forth. That should make him think."

"By gow!" says his mum, "make him think! It'll do more than that. It'll make him send for his Sworder there and then, and they'll have my head rolling on the floor before you can say 'Jack Robinson'!"

"All right, all right," says Aladdin, "I can see that it all looks a bit dodgy—but believe you me, it'll work out all right."

There was nothing she could say any more to persuade him, so she picked up the bowl and made her way down to the palace just as she was, in her moth-eaten widow's weeds.

When she got there, everything happened as Aladdin had predicted—except that she hung around in the audience-chamber all day and nobody took any notice of her. The Sultan did all the Sultan-ish things that he was there for, but the Wazirs and the chamberlains and the vergers paid no heed to the little old woman all in black with her baking-bowl.

The same thing happened the next day, and the next day, and the next, all the same for about a month, till Aladdin began to get a bit vexed. "What're you doing?" he said; "you're not trying. You must just be a bit more pushy."

Equally though, the Sultan was beginning to get more and more curious about this shabby, silent figure who kept turning up day by day. "Who is she?" he asked the Grand Wazir, "what does she want? If she's here tomorrow see that she's called before me."

Accordingly, next day, no one was more surprised, or flustered, than Mrs Tuanki when she was called up to the Sultan first off. "Oh my Lord," she said, kissing the ground in front of him, "Oh my Lord, Allah bless thee, and Allah forgive me, but I have a boon to ask which is for thine ears only. Hear me, and then too grant me forgiveness."

"Very well," said the Sultan, "if it's something that Allah can forgive then I'm sure I can too," and turning to the Grand Wazir he said, "Clear the court!"

Grumbling mightily the folk in the audience-chamber were cleared back to the street; the courtiers went out, and Aladdin's mum was left confronting the Sultan and the Grand Wazir who stayed as his chief adviser. "So what's all the fuss about?" asked the Sultan, and Aladdin's mum entered into the whole story about how Aladdin was wasting away for love of the Sultan's daughter and had sent her along to ask for her hand in marriage.

The Sultan was so astounded by the cheek of this proposal, coming from such a decrepit old woman, that the only thing he could do was laugh. "In the name of Allah," he cried, "we are a noble nation that even a tailor's widow may seek a Princess for a daughter-in-law—and I suppose that's your wedding present in there," pointing to the baking-bowl.

"Well as it happens, my Lord, it is," said Mrs Tuanki, much relieved that the Sultan was taking everything so matily, and she pulled the blue-check cloth off the baking-bowl. Wow! Red, green, blue, silver, gold, the jewels shone out with amazing radiance, turning the audience-chamber into a gallery that danced with colour. Aladdin's mum (who hadn't been expecting anything quite like that) fell over backwards with surprise and the Sultan and his Grand Wazir leapt out of their chairs for fear the whole brilliant vessel might there and then explode.

"Madam," said the Sultan, when he'd come back to his senses, "Madam; allow me to pay mind to this present of yours," and he began to examine the contents of the bowl with some care, picking out gems of especial magnificence and seeing, with a practised eye, that this baking-bowl held more treasure than the treasury of his own palace. Plainly the son of this decrepit widow was a person to be reckoned with, and if he had more jewels where these came from, he would make a match for the Princess Badr al-Budur beyond that of any other suitor.

That was the trouble, though. For before Mrs Tuanki ever appeared on the

scene the Sultan's Grand Wazir had made approaches to his Lord in the interests of his son, and it was all but settled that this young chap was going to marry the Princess—thus keeping all the monkeys together at the top of the tree. But the Wazir's son was not likely to come up with courting-presents like Aladdin's and the Sultan was bothered to know how he could keep his Wazir happy and get his hands on the jewellery.

"Madam," he said again (can't you just hear him!), "we are honoured to be seen as worthy to receive a gift of this ethereal splendour, and honoured that the giver should think so highly of us that he seeks the hand of our daughter in marriage. How could we refuse? But I fear that we cannot accede to your request with absolute spontaneity, for you must know that the Princess Badr al-Budur is just now engaged in a religious retreat, and nothing can be done until her return in three months' time. Pray tell your son, the honourable Messire Aladdin, that we shall convey the treasure of his heart and of his house to our daughter and shall await a prosperous engagement when our daughter shall return."

Bridegroom Number One

"I don't like it," said Mrs Tuanki when she got back home. "He's given us the brush-off and he's kept all those jewels. What was all that about a religious retreat? First time I ever heard of Princesses doing a thing like that . . ." But Aladdin didn't seem to mind. "You told him," he said; "you gave him the present. He knows what's what. We'll just wait and see what happens." So wait they did.

But although the Sultan had said what he said in order to gain time, he'd reckoned without the persistence of the Grand Wazir. That one wasn't going to see his son lose out to some inconsequential peasant. So he kept on at the Sultan (he was good at keeping on, that was one of the things he was paid for), and so it turned out that the Sultan began to think that the bowlful of jewels was a simple piece of good fortune and that his daughter really ought to marry the Wazir's son. Why not? It had always seemed a good idea. Let's get on with it.

So one day, a couple of months after her audience with the Sultan, Aladdin's mum went down to the town and was startled to see flags flying and bunting in the streets. "What's going on here, then?" she asked; and they told her that the Wazir's son was getting betrothed to the Sultan's daughter. "Where've you been then, missus?" they said. "Haven't you heard about that already?"

Without more ado, Mrs Tuanki went back to Aladdin and told him the news. "I never did trust those folk," he said, "but don't you mind. I've not done with them yet," and he sat quietly at home while everyone in town got drunk. That evening, when they'd all gone to bed, he went into his room and rubbed the Lamp. Flash! there was the Jinni. "I am the Slave of the Lamp!" he roared, "and of all who hold the Lamp; command me and all my fellows to whatever you desire. Speak!" So Aladdin spoke and told him what he was to do: he was to go and fetch the Princess Badr al-Budur and the Wazir's son on their bridal couch, he was to dump the Wazir's son in the bog out back and keep guard over him for the night, then in the morning he was to take them and the couch back to the Sultan's palace.

All this the Jinni accomplished. Aladdin spent the night moonstruck by the sleeping Princess, the Wazir's son spent the night getting cold cramps in the bog, and next day they found themselves back at the palace in time for breakfast. "Well that was a funny dream," said the Princess, and told her mum what had happened; but the Wazir's son sat shivering and said nothing at all.

Next night the same thing happened. The Princess and the Wazir's son had hardly got to bed before the Jinni came again and dumped the boy in the bog and the girl in the room in front of Aladdin's adoring gaze. Then back to the palace for breakfast. This time the Wazir's son spoke up. "I've had enough of this," he said, "if it's someone's idea of a joke they can try it on another muggins in the future," and he went back home and refused to go on with the marriage. The Grand Wazir did all he could to persuade him to change his mind—because, after all, the Princess Badr al-Budur was a pretty good catch—but the lad was so clemmed with the damp-cold and so frightened of the Jinni that he decided the Heavens were against the whole match.

As for the Princess, she still thought that it had all been a dream—but not by any means as offensive as the Wazir's son made out.

Bridegroom Number Two

With all the excitement over the wedding and everything that happened after, the Sultan had quite forgotten his promise to Aladdin's mother. But of course she'd not forgotten—nor Aladdin neither—and when the three months were up from the day she'd handed over the jewels, she went back to the audience-chamber in the Palace and waited to see the Sultan.

This time though, she didn't have to wait long. No sooner did the Sultan see this little bitty woman in her raggety gown than he remembered what had happened and he called over his Grand Wazir for a hasty confabulation. "Look who's there," he whispered, "you know what she's come for. What are we going to do about that?"

Now the Grand Wazir was still sore about his son backing out of the marriage, and he certainly wasn't keen for anyone else to step in—least of all these people. "Easy, my Lord," he said, "all you have to do is ask for more dowry. Tell her that everything can be arranged but that you'll need—er—hem—um" (counting on his fingers), "forty more bowls of jewellery like the last lot. That should settle her."

So the Sultan called up Mrs Widow Tuanki, who straightway reminded him that this was the end of the three-month interval and hoped that his daughter was now finished with the religious retreat, being as how she should now be set to marry Aladdin. "Indeed, indeed, dear Madam," said the Sultan, "did you think we had forgotten? Why, all is now ready to be set in train—processions, ceremonies, feasts and so forth—and all we need is the rest of the dower-gifts."

"Eh?" said Aladdin's mum, "dower-gifts? That's the first I've heard of those. What does your Excellency have in mind?"

Well, the Sultan got the Grand Wazir to explain about the forty bowls of gemstones, and that gentleman threw in for good measure that they expected delivery to be made by forty white dancing girls, escorted by forty black body slaves, and all by tomorrow afternoon, if you please. What's more, he hoped the weather would keep fine for the wedding.

Aladdin's mum returned home all cast down. She didn't really understand how her boy had come by all those jewels in the first place, and she certainly didn't see how he could get any more—but she gave him the message none the less. "Fine," said Aladdin, "let's get on with it"; and he straightway went off to his room, rubbed the Lamp, and told the Jinni what had happened and what they had to do.

"I hear and obey, Master," said the Jinni, and before Mrs Tuanki could think straight there started up a grand procession from her house to the

[163]

Sultan's palace: forty dancing girls, each carrying an earthenware bowl of gems from the Hoard in the Garden, and each protected by a slave, walking beside her with a drawn scimitar. And very lovely they all looked too.

"Go on, Mum," said Aladdin, "go on with them. Give my best respects to the Sultan and tell him that I'll be along to marry the Princess in the morning—while the weather holds."

And so it came about. The Sultan and the Grand Wazir were just finishing the last of the day's business in the audience-chamber when they heard a great racket outside and in walked Aladdin's mum, still in her old robe, followed by the dancing girls with all the trinkets. The hall shone with their brightness, and Mrs Tuanki kneeled before the Sultan and said, "The wedding gifts, my Lord. My son Aladdin will be here tomorrow."

The Sultan was thunderstruck. The Grand Wazir turned green with rage. But there was nothing for it. What they'd asked for, they'd got, and for the second time that season they had to set about fixing a wedding for the Princess Badr al-Budur. (She, of course, didn't have any say in the matter, but she was glad enough to get away from the Wazir's son, whom she'd always thought was a bit of a weed, and she didn't think there could be much wrong with a newcomer who gave her bowlfuls of jewels for a present.)

The flags and the bunting were brought out again, and the next morning Aladdin set out in state to make himself known to his future father-in-law. He had called up the Slave of the Lamp before he left and this was the order of his train:

twenty-four Mamelukes with war-chargers and accoutrements;
Aladdin
on a white stallion, whose saddle and bridle were encrusted with gems;
twelve more Mamelukes with war-chargers and accoutrements;
forty-eight white slaves,
each carrying a bowl in which were a thousand gold pieces;
Aladdin's mum;
twelve handmaids clothed as the daughters of morning,
and all surrounded by a guard of honour,
crying:
"Praise to Allah! Praise to Him who Changeth and is not Changed!"

Admittedly it looked a bit like an army, but Aladdin had various of the Mamelukes and the slaves throw gold pieces in among the crowd as they travelled along the streets, so everybody blessed him for a proper gentleman, just right for their Princess.

When the procession eventually reached the Sultan's palace, Aladdin rode to the front and greeted the King with a pretty speech on the lines of him thanking the Sultan for agreeing to bestow his daughter on so humble a person . . . not being worthy of so precious a jewel . . . tongue-tied by so much honour . . . etc., etc., until the Sultan thought best to interrupt and suggest that they all went indoors for a cup of tea. This they did, and in the course of their further conversation Aladdin happened to remark that he was eager to build a little house or pavilion which might serve as a new home for his bride, and did the Sultan have any thoughts on the matter?

"Well," said the Sultan, "it so happens that there's a stretch of land opposite my palace there which we only use for practising polo on, why don't you build something there?"

"Very well then," said Aladdin, "I'll get that done, and then we can proceed with the wedding and so on," and with much bowing and arm-waving he left the room and took himself off to a quiet place. Here he pulled the Lamp from out of his wedding robes, rubbed it, and out sprang the Slave of the Lamp: "Speak, Lord! Command me and my fellows to whatever you may desire!" and Aladdin thereupon ordered the building of a pavilion that might be one of the wonders of the world:

Its outer stones were of jasper and alabaster, inlaid with marble and mosaic-work; within were chambers within chambers, each furnished to perfection, and containing proper stores of household utensils, and wardrobes of fine robes, and chests full of gold and silverware and caskets of bright gems; and there were kitchens and stables, all serviced with attendants and slaves, and over all there was a great belvedere, looking out over town and country, with twenty-four windows decorated with emeralds and rubies—except at one corner, and there, there was only plain plasterwork—unfinished.

All this Aladdin commanded, and in a trice it was done; whereupon Aladdin asked the Jinni to lay a carpet of gold-inwrought brocade from the door of his pavilion to the entrance of the Sultan's palace. Then he returned to the company and invited them to come and see the little house that he'd put up for his bride.

Well—between you and me—up till now they'd treated Aladdin as a bit of a joke. After all, he'd never tried to hide the fact that he was a tailor's son, and they all thought that he'd struck it lucky somehow or other but that it wouldn't last. When they came to the door of the palace though, and saw that gleaming new building rising up beyond the courtyard they were astounded.

"Wonderful . . . gorgeous . . . majestic," they all said to each other,

but the Grand Wazir said, "Sorcery! We are all at the mercy of the Prince of Darkness!"

"Well, we all know what you mean by that," said the Sultan, "you're still jealous because Aladdin's marrying my daughter instead of your son. Come on, let's go and look at this sorcery."

So with the Sultan in the lead they all trooped along the golden carpet to the door of the pavilion, where Aladdin formally greeted them and bade them welcome. Then he took the Sultan round the rooms of the house, disclosing all their comforts and treasures. Eventually they climbed to the belvedere with its sights across land and sea, and as the Sultan was marvelling at the opulence of it all, so he came to the window set in unadorned plaster. "Ho!" he said, "what of this then? Your builder seems to have missed a bit out."

"Too true," said Aladdin, "too true. But such was the speed that we worked, to please your Highness and the daughter of your Highness, we didn't have time to finish the building before your visit. It shall be done tomorrow."

"There you are then," said the Sultan, looking at the Grand Wazir, "what sort of sorcery is that if it can't finish the job properly? You impugn my son-in-law too readily." And he ordered his own architect and his own builders to complete the work on the window and gave signal for the festivities to begin, to celebrate the marriage of Aladdin to the Princess Badr al-Budur.

The Wizard

From that day on there seemed to be nothing that could spoil the good fortune and the happiness of Aladdin and his family. The Princess discovered that she liked her new husband even more than she liked the jewels that he kept producing; Aladdin's mum found housekeeping in the royal pavilion a good deal more agreeable than spinning in the back streets; and Aladdin himself struck up a chummy relationship with the Sultan and they used to go hunting and fishing and playing polo together when the Sultan wasn't having to give audiences and suchlike.

But we've forgotten about that Moorish magician who was the cause of all this in the first place (and that's not surprising, because Aladdin had forgotten about him too). Over in Africa though, the magician had not forgotten about Aladdin. He hadn't been home long before he began to be sorry that he'd lost his temper when he shut Aladdin in the cave—especially since he'd shut his Ring of Solomon in there too—and he began to ponder how he might make good some of his losses.

He got out all his sand-tables and stuff and he began to make some prognostications about what might be happening in China—and you can guess his surprise when he discovered that Aladdin was not only still alive but was now Master of the Slaves of the Lamp. He just about had a fit. "Exterminate him; exterminate him!" he yelled, stamping round the room and kicking his apparatus, "I shall not rest till I have encompassed his destruction."

Straightway he began to make his plans, and once again he set off for China. This time he had no need to comb the streets for his victim, because everyone was still talking about the Emir Aladdin, his pavilion of splendour, and his habit of throwing golden dinars around whenever he went for a walk. Indeed, you could see the belvedere of the pavilion, with its (now) twenty-four glittering windows, from every side of the town, and the wizard need only do a few simple spells with his sand-table to discover that the Lamp of Power was kept in the house and not carried about by Aladdin wherever he went.

"That has him," said the magician, and he set about obtaining a stock of brand-new copper lamps which he carefully packed in baskets for loading on to a donkey. When all was ready he waited till he heard news that Aladdin had gone out hunting, and then he started through the town like any trader in the streets. "New lamps!" he cried. "New lamps for old! Come on, ladies, do yourselves a favour, out with your old lamps; every old lamp gets a new one in exchange! Roll up, roll up! New lamps for old!"

Well, it wasn't long before half the city was following along behind him, pointing their fingers at him and calling everyone else to watch. "He's barmy," they shouted, "look at old barmy-boots! Go fetch your old lamps and get him to give you a new one!"

Before long the wizard made sure that he was in the street going past Aladdin's house, and with all the commotion, the Princess Badr al-Budur couldn't help sending to know if it was bloody revolution or what-all. "Oh, ma'am," said the servant coming back, "it's a mad African, giving away new lamps in exchange for old ones. Everyone's laughing at him. But—come to think of it—the Master's got a dirty old lamp, stuck away in his back room,

let's swap it and give him a surprise." Which is just what they did. They sent a slave down to the street to change Aladdin's old lamp for a new one and as soon as he'd done so the magician discerned that the Lamp of Power was now in his hands. "Take the lot, you idiots! Take the lot!" he cried, and he tipped the donkey-baskets all over the road, and while everyone rushed up to see what they could find he made off into the side streets round the back.

When he'd got clear of the crowds and into a deserted part of the town, the wizard sat down to wait for nightfall, and then he rubbed the Lamp. Shezam! out came the Jinni. "Speak! I am the Slave of the Lamp; command me and all my fellows to whatever you desire!"

"Well, it's good to meet you after all this time," said the wizard, "here's what I want," and he commanded the Slave of the Lamp to uproot Aladdin's pavilion and all that was in it and to carry the lot (with the magician included) back to his estates in Africa. "Hearing and obeying!" said the Jinni, and straightway the whole caboodle was magicked off to Africa, leaving nothing but the polo practice-ground in front of the Sultan's palace.

In the morning, when he woke up, the Sultan did what he usually did and drew the curtains to look across at Aladdin's pavilion. And there it was—gone. He closed his eyes, and opened them again slowly. Still gone. So he sent for the Grand Wazir. "What's happened then?" he asked.

"Wha'd'you mean 'what's happened then?'" asked the Wazir, who'd only just woken up.

"Where is it?" asked the Sultan.

"Where's what?" asked the Wazir.

"That," said the Sultan, and he pointed out of the window.

The Wazir gulped. "Well, it was there last night . . . and . . . and . . . oh! Excellency," (wringing his hands) "isn't that what I've said all along? It's sorcery. We've all been duped by sorcerers!"

This time the Sultan was more inclined to believe his Grand Wazir— especially since he'd now lost his daughter—but it wasn't long before he discovered that Aladdin hadn't been in the pavilion but had gone off hunting. "Very well," he said, "he must be arrested. Guards! . . ." and he called up the captain of the guard and ordered him to go and hunt Aladdin and to bring him back a prisoner. The fellow was a sorcerer and would have his head chopped off.

The captain of the guard was surprised about this because, like everyone else, he'd always found the Emir Aladdin a sociable sort of chap, as unsorcerer-like as they come. But Sultan's orders were Sultan's orders, so he took his men into the forests and before long they'd found Aladdin and taken him back to the palace, a prisoner. He marched up to the Sultan's room:

[170]

tramp, tramp, tramp! "Now," said the Sultan, "what's the meaning of this?" and he pointed out of the window to where Aladdin's pavilion wasn't. Aladdin looked and, like the Sultan and Wazir before him, looked again. Polo practice-ground; nothing else.

"Your Highness," said Aladdin, "I don't know. To be sure, everything was there when I went away, how should I know what's become of it?"

"Well, it's your house," said the Sultan, "you ought to look after it; and that thing on your neck is your head, and you ought to look after that too. If you can't find your house and my daughter in the next six months I'll have it put on a pole by the city gate."

"Six months," cried Aladdin, "six months! Good grief! If I can't find them all in the next six weeks I'll chop my head off myself and bring it to you as a present."

So they let Aladdin go and he began to wander round in a disconsolate sort of way, pondering how a place that size could have vanished and how he could set about finding it. And as it turned out, his ramblings led him to the self-same valley where he'd had the adventure with the treasure cave and that suddenly reminded him about his Ring, blessed with the power of Solomon

himself. So without more ado he rubbed the Ring, there on his finger, and out came the Jinni: "Speak! I am the Slave of the Ring; speak and tell me your desires!"

"Slave of the Ring," said Aladdin, "my house is vanished, my wife is vanished, find them and bring them back to the place of their proper abode."

"Alas!" said the Jinni, "that may not be. These things are beyond my competence, for they are now in the power of the Slave of the Lamp. I dare not attempt it."

"Very well," said Aladdin, "in that case take me to my house."

"I hear and obey," said the Jinni, and in the space of an eye-glance he set Aladdin down beside his pavilion in Africa. There he was, just under the window of the Princess Badr al-Budur.

Hardly had Aladdin staggered to his feet and settled that this was, indeed, his house when the Princess's window opened and the Princess's maidservant put her head out to get some fresh air. She spotted this Chinese-looking chap down below and nearly fell out of the window as she recognized Aladdin. "O my lady! O my lady!" she called back into the room, "here's my Lord Aladdin standing in the garden!" The Princess rushed up to the window, and when she saw that it certainly was Aladdin, she threw down one of her bracelets from her wrist so that he looked up at her. "Round the back!" she called at him in a sort of whisper. "Go through the little door round the back!" and she sent the maidservant down to bring Aladdin to her room.

Apparently the wizard was at that time doing some shopping in an African city down the road, so Aladdin and the Princess Badr al-Budur were able to have a long talk about the peculiar things that had happened. "Tell me," said Aladdin, by way of a start, "have you come across an old copper lamp that I used to keep round at the back of my room?"

"Oh," said the Princess, "don't talk about that. We took it down to the street to a hawker who was swapping old lamps for new ones, and now it's got into the hands of the Maghrabi—the Accursed One—who brought us here, and he treasures it as the source of all Power. He carries it about with him all the time, tucked down the inside of his robe."

When he heard that, Aladdin understood everything, and saw what now had to be done. It seemed that ever since they'd made their instantaneous journey to Africa, the Princess and the magician had been at daggers drawn, because he would keep on trying to persuade her that Aladdin was dead and she'd best marry him and have done with it, while she reckoned she knew different and wasn't going to have any truck with a trickster anyway.

What Aladdin now suggested was that she should appear to change her mind—give up on the idea that her man was still alive and offer a bit of encouragement to the wizard. Then, if she could inveigle him into having a drink with her, she could spike his liquor and they'd have a fair chance of getting back the Lamp. And Aladdin went off to where his old room used to be, dug around in a cabinet and came back with a couple of white pills. "Crush those up and put them in his glass," he said, "they'll do the trick."

And that's what happened. When the wizard came back from the shops Aladdin hid behind a curtain and the Princess Badr al-Budur got herself up to look all sexy. "Why don't you come up and see me some time this evening?" she said to the magician, "I'm tired of being cooped up here all on my own; I could do with some company."

Well, a nod's as good as a wink to a blind man, so they say, and the wizard was quite taken in by this apparent change of heart. (He'd always had a high opinion of himself, and couldn't see why the Princess hadn't fallen for him first off anyway.) So that evening he smartened himself up and came up to the Princess's apartments for some supper, while the Princess, for her part, made sure that everything was comfy and there was plenty to drink.

Oh dear, you fellows who're listening to this story, let it be a lesson to you all. She waggled her hips at the old chap, in her silken trousers; she flashed her eyes at him over her flimsy veil—and she kept on pouring. From a state of

delight, to a state of euphoria, he went on tipping back his glass until he was eventually almost catatonic and could hardly have got his hands on her if he'd tried. Then it was that she slipped the crushed powder into his drink and he keeled over for good.

Out from behind the curtain came Aladdin, with a dagger in his hand. They fished around inside the wizard's robe till they found where he'd tucked away the Lamp, and when they'd got it out and made sure it was the right one, Aladdin shoved the dagger into his ribs and put an end to his wizardry forever.

How It Ended

You might think that there's not much more to be said. You might think that all we need to do is to tell how Aladdin once more summoned the Slave of the Lamp, ordered him to take the house back to where it started from, and how the Sultan—waking up next morning—was as surprised to see the pavilion back on the polo-ground as he had been to see it vanish. Obviously he was delighted to have his daughter home again, and was all ready to forgive and forget—so you might think that they all lived happily ever after. But you'd be wrong.

You see the African magician had a brother, who was a pretty good wizard on his own account. They never saw much of each other, but they liked to keep in touch at Christmas, as it were, and the brother began to get a bit agitated when the usual greetings never turned up. So he got his own set of sand-tables and magical instruments and he did a bit of conjuring—and what did he discover but that his brother had been murdered and his body carried off to China, to the city of all cities.

"Vengeance is mine," said Wizard Number Two—or words to that effect—and he straightway set out for China to see what he could do about it. He travelled long weeks and months over the seas and the mountains and finally ended up outside the city in what was called 'the Strangers' Khan', a kind of hostelry for foreigners. Here he began his investigations to find out more about his brother's murderer and ways to get at him, and he had the good fortune one day to hear some dominoes-players in a nearby tavern talking about the Holy Fatimah. Apparently this Holy Fatimah was a saintly hermitess from the mountains, who'd been causing quite a stir lately with various acts of piety and healing, and she was due to be coming to town soon to bless, and be blessed by, the Sultan and his family. So the wizard found out where she lived—up in a little cave above the city—and set off to visit her.

He arrived at the cave, as he'd planned, round about night-time and he waited on guard there till early next morning, when he went inside and found the hermitess just waking up. Before she could say anything he pulled out his dagger and forced her there and then to change clothes with him, or else . . . When he'd done that he made her fetch her staff and her other gear and he got her to show him how she went about her ministrations—and when he'd done that, and got it all off pat, he asked her for a rope for a girdle, and that he used to hang her with. Just like that. He hanged her there in the cave and then threw her body into a nearby pit. So much for wizards. . .

Once he'd got rid of the Holy Fatimah he went down to the city in her cloak, and with her veil covering his beard and his mustachios, and he made for the Sultan's palace. Before he got there though, there was so much commotion, with everybody in the street wanting a benediction or a Touch, that he attracted the attention of the Princess Badr al-Budur, who asked her maid to bring him straight into the house.

This, of course, was just what he wanted. Imitating the Holy Fatimah he behaved all smarmy (said he wouldn't take anything to eat because he was fasting, but really because he was worried about someone seeing his whiskers), and he let her show him around the pavilion. Everywhere they went he gave the right sort of gasps of astonishment, but when at last they got to the belvedere on the roof he allowed himself a sigh of disappointment. "Oh, dear!" he said, "such a beautiful room, but spoiled for want of a last perfection."

"What do you mean?" asked the Princess, "'spoiled for want of a last perfection'; what could possibly make the place more perfect?"

"Ah," said the Fatimah Wizard, "what you need here—right in the middle of the ceiling—is a Rukh's egg. They're not easy to come by. They belong to the largest birds in the world. But a Rukh's egg, hanging there from the middle of the ceiling . . . perfect!"

Well, the Princess Badr al-Badur was pretty upset about this, and after she'd sent Fatimah off to have a rest before meeting the Sultan, she sent for Aladdin. "What's the trouble?" says he.

"Duff!" says she. "A duff job. You set about building the smartest place in the kingdom and you don't finish it off properly. Where's the Rukh's egg that ought to be hanging from the ceiling?" and she explained to him about the visit from Fatimah and what the old girl had said.

"Don't worry!" said Aladdin. "If it wasn't done then it can surely be done now," and he went off to his room, got out the Lamp and rubbed it. Flash! back came the Jinni. "Speak! I am the Slave of the Lamp! Command me and all my fellows to whatever you desire!"

"Well," said Aladdin, "what I want you to do is to fetch me the egg of a bird

called a Rukh and hang it from the dome of my belvedere.''

''Zambahshalamahzarúska!'' roared the Jinni, and Aladdin collapsed on to
the floor, ''what insolent ingratitude is this? Have not we Slaves of the Lamp
done all your biddings? Furnished your processions? Filled your bowls with
gold? Built your mansion—and carried it backwards and forwards over the
earth? Was that not enough, that you must now ask us to fetch our Mistress
of Heaven and hang her up in your pleasure-dome? By Allah, I am minded
to turn you to ashes and scatter you to the twelve quarters of the wind.
Command me no more such commands.'' And the Jinni went back into
the Lamp.

When Aladdin had recovered a little, and got up off the floor, he began to
ponder why the Holy Fatimah should have made this suggestion which had so
nearly brought about their downfall. What could she know of Rukhs' eggs?
More than that—what could she know of Jann who had this intimate
relationship with Rukhs' eggs?

So when he went downstairs he told the Princess, his wife, that he'd like to see the Holy Fatimah because he'd suddenly come over all queer, with a bad headache (which was not too far from the truth). The Princess sent for the hermitess, who should have finished her rest by now, and when the Fatimah Wizard came into the room and saw Aladdin standing there, he realized that all his schemes were moving to success. He went over to Aladdin, feeling in his robe as though to bring out some charm against headaches, but really palming his own dagger. Aladdin watched him with his eyes well open, and as the Holy Lady raised her arm he grabbed it by the wrist, twisted, and, when the dagger fell to the floor . . . picked it up and drove it through the robes and into the heart of the Moorish Wizard.

"Yow!" yelled the Princess; "Screech!" yelled the Princess's servants; but Aladdin stuck his foot on Fatimah's chest, pulled out the dagger, and then tore away the veiling so that everyone could see the Holy Woman's beard and mustachios. "All thanks to Allah and the Rukh's egg," said Aladdin; and now that Wizard One and Wizard Two were both out of the way Aladdin, and Aladdin's wife, and Aladdin's mum, and the Sultan and all the population of the city of cities (except possibly the Grand Wazir), lived happily ever after.

With the ending of this story of Aladdin the first sunbeam touched the minarets of the Sultan's palace and Sheherezade knew that for a thousand nights and one night she had been winning the mind and heart of the Shah Shahryar. Through all this time she had loved him—had borne him three boy-children—and through all this time at the behest of her sister Dunyazad she had told him story upon story. But now, as the dawn broke, she silenced the pleas of Dunyazad, rose to her feet and, kissing the ground before the King, she said: "Lord of the time and of the age, I am thy handmaid. For a thousand nights and one night I have entertained thee with tales and legends, jests and moral instances, and now I crave a boon of thee!"

And the King said, "Ask, O Sheherezade, and it shall be granted unto thee."

Whereupon she cried: "Bring me my children!" And when the nurses and eunuchs had brought the children before the King she said: "O King of the age, these are thy children and I crave that thou release me from the doom of thy judgement, that I may rear them fittingly as they should be reared."

Then the King answered: "O Sheherezade, I pardoned thee before the coming of these children for I found thee to be most candid and most fair. Allah bless thee all thy days and may He witness against me that I exempt thee from aught that can harm thee." And with these words he called for his Wazirs and Emirs and for the Officers of the Crown and decreed that there should be public feasting to celebrate the marriage of the Shah Shahryar to Sheherezade. And in like way his brother, the Shah Zaman, who had ever been attendant upon his actions, besought that he might marry Dunyazad, so thus it came about that, amid rejoicings which no storyteller may describe, the two brothers were united to the two sisters and they dwelt together in all solace and contentment until there came to them the Destroyer of delights, the Sunderer of societies and the Garnerer of graveyards.

So
Glory be to Him
whom the Shifts of Time waste not away;
and
Prayer and Peace
upon the Chosen One among his creatures
the Lord Mohammed
through whom we supplicate for a goodly and godly

END

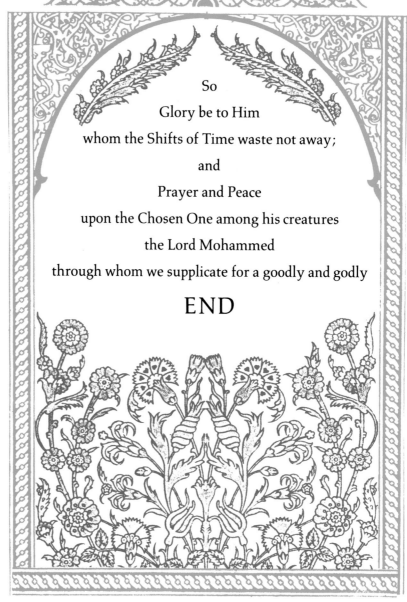

EDITOR'S REMARKS

To call a book 'The Arabian Nights' is very much to over-simplify a complicated subject. For there is no such thing—neither in Arabic or Persian, nor in French nor English. What we call 'The Arabian Nights' is a huge collection of stories that were set into the framework of the tale of Sheherezade—but if you want to try to settle what exactly those stories were you will need the help of the Slave of the Lamp and the lifetime of a Sage.

The trouble is that these stories, attributed to Sheherezade, are to be found in various ancient manuscripts and that these manuscripts differ from each other both as to the number of stories they include and the versions of the stories that are told. To make matters worse, the real interest in 'The Arabian Nights' as a printed book lay not in Arabia at all, but in Europe, where an explosion of interest occurred once Antoine Galland started to publish his French translation in 1704 (which was quickly translated into English too). These European translations were themselves very different from the Arabian manuscripts—not least because Europeans were coy about printing stories where grown men wet their trousers or where everyone enjoyed making love to everyone else—so that a collection of 'Nights' appeared which did not correspond very closely to that of the original Arabian ones.

(Especially odd is the history of the versions of the two best-known stories in the whole collection: *Ali Baba* and *Aladdin*. Neither of these tales is to be found in the authentic Arabian mss. Both were translated by Galland from a quite separate source, which has never been fully elucidated. He apparently noted the tales while they were being told by a Maronite storyteller in Europe.)

But if we cannot say for sure what 'The Arabian Nights' are, we all have some idea of what they ought to be—exotic tales of magic or passion told over a thousand and one nights by a lady who was anxious not to have her head chopped off. The hope behind this present book is that it will give a satisfying form to that idea: that it will show something of the character and variety of the tales and also preserve the impression of

Sheherezade's storytelling stamina. (That is not altogether easy in a book that is a mere 192 pages long, when the original may be anything up to three thousand.)

In trying to carry out this aim I have worked in cheerful ignorance of all the linguistic and anthropological scholarship that ought to be brought to bear on a proper translation of 'The Arabian Nights', but I have tried always to show respect for the business of storytelling. I have chosen as a base for my adaptation the nineteenth century translation of John Payne, as refurbished and augmented by Sir Richard Burton in the sixteen volumes of his 'Nights' and 'Supplemental Nights' (1885–1888). I have however hacked and hewn at the stories in a manner that would have appalled that fiery gentleman, in order to try to create a consistent, small-scale replica of the original. No doubt many modern Arabists will deplore this reversion to what has been called 'richly upholstered Victorian prose'. I would choose to argue though that, for many English readers, such prose well represents the exoticism that is expected of these Oriental stories and that its formalities and rotundities separate it from the direct colloquialism that we enjoy in European folk tales. Amidst all the 'thee-ing' and 'thou-ing' I have still sought to preserve a prose rhythm which will sound right if the stories are told—as Sheherezade told them—aloud to an audience. Mine be the head that is lopped off if everyone falls asleep.

The Text

A few notes are given below on the stories that have been re-told in full, although the reader will have noticed that various other stories are mentioned in order to give the impression of the nights going by. The tales are roughly in the sequence in which they appear in Burton, but I have not hesitated to move them around in the interests of giving this book what I hope appears a satisfactory shape.

The Tales: sequence, sources and so on

The Frame Story: The practice of using a story as an excuse for telling more stories is of ancient descent, perhaps originating with the Buddhist *Jatakas* of the third century before Christ. Without doubt though the frame story of the two Shahs is the most famous example of the device and, as I have already said, I believe that even a short sequence of the stories should preserve the references to Sheherezade as storyteller.

In this version therefore I have set out fairly fully the events that led up to Sheherezade's marathon endeavour, including the characteristic story-within-a-story when the Shah Shahryar and his brother set off in search of a woman more faithless than their own wretched consorts. (This motif has later parallels in such European comic tales as the Grimms' 'Clever Elsie', or the English 'The Three Sillies', where a wooer will only claim his foolish bride when he finds three people more stupid than she.)

Sheherezade is often left out of abbreviated versions of *The Arabian Nights* or else—as in Galland—the night-by-night sequence is abandoned because it makes for too many interruptions. Nevertheless, despite the extreme variations in the length and complexity of the stories which Sheherezade tells, her submerged presence gives a unifying interest to the collection. She holds its disparate contents together rather as the Baghdad bag was deemed by the Kurdish man to contain so many diverse wonders (see page 73). Furthermore, Sheherezade's presence as originating storyteller helps to emphasize one of the narrative tricks of the *Nights*: the tendency which people within her stories have to introduce additional anecdotes of their own to illustrate a point which they wish to make, so that stories occur within stories like a series of Chinese boxes.

Notable early instances of the appearance of frame-stories in European literature are Boccaccio's *Decameron* (1348–1353), Chaucer's *Canterbury Tales* (1380–1400), and Basile's *Pentamerone* (1634–1636) where the frame surrounds a collection of some fifty folk tales. In these examples the use of the frame probably arises from the author's liking for it as a narrative device rather than from any direct influence from the then-unpublished and far more complex *Arabian Nights*.

The Fisherman and the Jinni (Burton, Nights 3–6). One of the most ancient stories in the collection, of which only the first half is given here. After the Jinni leaves the Fisherman the narrative swerves off into the barely-related and rather sadistic 'Tale of the Ensorcelled Prince' which has to do with the peculiar nature of the fish which the Fisherman catches. The exemplary tales of the Sage Duban, the Loyal Falcon, and the Faithful Parrot are nice examples of the use of story-within-story but I have changed their sequence in order to move from the darker to the lighter narratives. The parrot story is one of a large number about the bird found all over the world. In England an anecdote slightly similar to the one here was recorded in 1914, when the parrot was deemed a liar because it talked about 'the day it rained beans and bacon' after the cook had thrown the dinner at it.

Although 'The Fisherman and the Jinni' is Oriental to the core, some motifs are also found independently in European folklore: the fisherman who draws up a magic flounder, for instance, in the Grimms' 'Fisherman and his Wife', and the tricking of the Jinni which has an equivalent in the cat's trickery of the ogre in 'Puss-in-Boots'. A story reprinted in Sidney Hartland's *English Fairy and Other Folk Tales* (1890) even has a quick-witted fellow called Tommy persuade a ghost to get into a brandy-bottle which he corks up tight and throws in the river.

The Tale of the Hunchback (Burton, Nights 25–34). Another quintessentially Oriental construction which I have abridged by removing a quantity of the interpolated stories. These often lack what a Western reader would regard as point and they seriously delay the hunchback's resurrection.

The Fable of the Birds and the Beasts and the Carpenter (Burton, Nights 146–147). This and the following two stories are taken from some of the many short fables which appear in the *Nights*. As might be expected, these are less specific in their setting and in their application than are the longer 'Eastern' stories.

The Fable of the Wolf and the Fox (Burton, Nights 148–150).
The antagonism between wolf and fox is a standard theme in fable literature; here it has had superimposed upon it a fairly elaborate re-working of the well incident from Aesop's 'Fox and the Goat'. I have omitted a distracting internal story about a falcon and a partridge, and I have supplied a concluding sentence of my own which is intended to round off the fable more pointedly than in the original.

The Fable of the Mongoose and the Mouse (Burton, Night 150). In Burton the cunning thief of the fable is an ichneumon. I have replaced him with his more pronounceable relative.

The Tale of the Ebony Horse (Burton, Nights 357–371). The story is one of those told to Galland by his Maronite friend, and is thought to be of Persian origin, but I have introduced into it (p. 70) a slanderous remark at the expense of Persians taken from Burton's notes. The theme of aerial flight in pursuit of a princess is re-worked by Hans Christian Andersen in one of his funniest *eventyr*: 'The Flying Trunk'.

The Tale Told by Ali the Persian (Burton, Nights 294–295). Along with short fables, *The Arabian Nights* also includes many moral or comic anecdotes, some of which appear in the following sequence of stories. The absurd tale which Ali here tells to Harun Al-Rashid is a piece of Persian nonsense worthy of Edward Lear; I have however curtailed the storyteller's over-zealous listing of possible contents for the bag in the interests of a brisk ending.

Ma'an Bin-Zaidah, the Donkey and the Cucumbers (Burton, Night 271). As often happens with these little jokey stories, the Arabian narrator seems more interested in the progression of events than in what Westerners would see as 'a rounded conclusion'. I have therefore tinkered with some of the minor details of this tale in order to give it a slightly sharper edge.

The Story of Sindbad the Porter and Sindbad the Sailor (Burton, Nights 536–566). The extensive journeyings of Sindbad the Sailor 'as told to' Sindbad the Porter make up a

frame-story within the larger frame-story of the *Nights*. Its origins however are uncertain and it belongs as much to 'Odyssey' literature, or to the genre of travellers' tales, as it does to Orientalia. (In Sindbad's Third Voyage there is even a ferocious version of the Cyclops story in Homer.) Despite various colourful incidents the full panoply of Sindbad's seven voyages takes on a rather repetitive character when transcribed in full. I have therefore selected three of his most celebrated encounters which I hope will give sufficient indication of the mixture of fantasy and adventure which characterizes his adventures.

As you may guess, 'Sindbad' figures alongside 'Ali Baba' and 'Aladdin' as one of the three most popular stories in the whole of the *Nights*.

The Tale of the City of Brass (Burton, Nights 566–578). A story which makes double use of one of the most potent images of *The Arabian Nights*: palaces and cities in the grip of desertion and death. Indeed the family of King Ad did not have much luck in the architectural business, for just as the Black Castle (built by Kush, son of Shaddad, son of Ad) was wasted, so too was the city of many-pillared Iram (built by Shaddad himself) as recounted by Sheherezade during nights 275–279, although it does make a fitful reappearance as part of the Persian's luggage in 'The Tale which Ali the Persian Told' (p. 76).

The Man Who Stole the Dog's Golden Dish (Burton, Nights 340–341). An exemplary anecdote whose sober conclusion has no clear parallel in Western fables.

The Tale of the Ruined Man and his Dream (Burton, Nights 351–352). Sheherezade here tells a story the like of which is found in a multitude of versions in many parts of the world. In England the best-known retelling is 'The Pedlar of Swaffham'.

The Tale of the Simpleton and his Donkey (Burton, Night 388). An example of a 'noodle story', that genre which celebrates the comic behaviour of foolish people in many other places as well as Arabia.

The Tale of Ja'afar the Barmecide and the Ailing Bedouin
(Burton, Nights 394–395). Another piece of Lear-like
nonsense, but with a pay-off that would not have been
appreciated by Lear's contemporaries. Breaking wind in times
of stress is nonetheless recognized by Sheherezade, or rather
by Burton, as a natural human reaction and indeed, in the story
'How Abu Hasan Broke Wind' (Night 410) she perceives its
tragic consequences, since Abu Hasan exiled himself for ten
years following an embarrassing indiscretion, only to discover
that the event had been permanently recorded in his
home-town's calendar. (Edward de Vere, Earl of Oxford was
not much luckier. According to Aubrey he too was so ashamed
of farting before his Queen that—like Abu Hasan—"he went to
Travell, 7 years". On his return though "the Queen welcomed
him home, and sayd, My Lord, I had forgott the Fart".)

The Story of Ali Baba and the Forty Thieves (Burton,
Supplemental Nights 625–638). As I have mentioned above,
this story, along with 'Aladdin', is notable both for its
outstanding popularity and for its obscure origins. Because of
the uncertainty surrounding their existence as authentic
Arabian tales I have taken the licence to treat Burton's texts
more freely and to give a rather more colloquial tang to the
retelling of both stories.

I assume that the popularity of 'Ali Baba' led to the adoption
of some of the story's motifs into European folk literature.
Thus the first part of the tale is replicated in Grimms'
'Simeliberg', while the trick with the scales appears in such
stories as the Irish 'Hudden and Dudden and Donald O'Neary'
and the cognate Danish tale from which Hans Christian
Andersen derived 'Big Claus and Little Claus'.

The Story of Aladdin and the Slave of the Lamp (Burton,
Supplemental Nights 514–590). See the above note. Aladdin's
family name is not given in Burton and I have authenticated it
from a source in Drury Lane. As with 'Ali Baba', part of this
story has almost certainly found its way into the European
tradition through such tales as the Grimms' 'The Blue Light' and
Hans Christian Andersen's cognate 'The Tinder Box', both of
which also incorporate the door-marking motif from 'Ali Baba'.